To renew this book, phone 0845 1202811 or visit
our website at www.libcat.oxfordshire.gov.uk
You will need your library PIN number
(available from your library)

'This is a two-bedroom apartment? Only two bedrooms?'

Tess hoped that the squeak she could hear in her voice was just being distorted through the layers of confusion in her brain.

'It's okay, Tess. I'll sleep on the couch. It's perfectly comfortable.'

Tess felt a wave of relief wash over her as she sagged against the doorjamb. In fact she felt a little silly at her reaction, which could be seen as being slightly over the top. But, honestly, sharing the apartment with Fletch was bad enough—she didn't even want to contemplate sharing a bed with him.

She already knew how good that was.

And guilt had driven all the good out of her a lot of years ago.

'I think you're going to need to get yourself some clothes,' Fletch said as he plucked her overnight bag from her fingers and strode across his room, dumping it on his bed.

She nodded. 'I hadn't exactly planned on staying. I'll slip down in the next couple of days and pick up a few outfits.'

His eyes met hers as he tried not to think about the time she'd dragged him into a changing room on a slow Sunday morning and had her way with him in front of three mirrors.

He failed.

And if the sudden smoulder in her eyes was anything to go by so did she.

Dear Reader,

The subject matter of this book is a difficult one. The death of a child and the often paralysing grief that comes with it aren't exactly ripe for a romance novel. But in my line of work, I have unfortunately seen many couples go through this harrowing experience and I so often wonder how they fare when they leave the surrealness of the hospital setting and have to get on with their lives without the little person that completed it so utterly. From this Tess and Fletch were born, two people whose profound grief had driven them apart despite their love for each other.

My life has been charmed until recently, with no bereavements or tragedies to speak of. Then half way through 2011 I lost my mother quite unexpectedly. Needless to say I now have more than a passing acquaintance with grief. It's not the loss of a child but grief doesn't discriminate and it's been a long, hard road to trudge.

Giving Tess and Fletch their HEA, even a decade after the tragic events that had marked theirs lives, was vital for me on many fronts.

I hope you root for them as I did during their journey back to each other.

Regards,

Amy

HOW TO MEND A
BROKEN HEART

BY
AMY ANDREWS

For Carita. Who knows.

First published in Great Britain 2012
by Mills & Boon, an imprint of Harlequin (UK) Limited.
Harlequin (UK) Limited, Eton House, 18-24 Paradise Road,
Richmond, Surrey TW9 1SR

© Alison Ahearn 2012

ISBN: 978 0 263 22782 6

Harlequin (UK) policy is to use papers that are natural, renewable and recyclable products and made from wood grown in sustainable forests. The logging and manufacturing process conform to the legal environmental regulations of the country of origin.

Printed and bound in Great Britain
by CPI Antony Rowe, Chippenham, Wiltshire

Amy Andrews has always loved writing, and still can't quite believe that she gets to do it for a living. Creating wonderful heroines and gorgeous heroes and telling their stories is an amazing way to pass the day. Sometimes they don't always act as she'd like them to—but then neither do her kids, so she's kind of used to it. Amy lives in the very beautiful Samford Valley, with her husband and aforementioned children, along with six brown chooks and two black dogs.

She loves to hear from her readers. Drop her a line at www.amyandrews.com.au

Recent titles by the same author:

SYDNEY HARBOUR HOSPITAL: LUCA'S BAD GIRL
WAKING UP WITH DR OFF-LIMITS
JUST ONE LAST NIGHT…
RESCUED BY THE DREAMY DOC
VALENTINO'S PREGNANCY BOMBSHELL
ALESSANDRO AND THE CHEERY NANNY

**These books are also available in eBook format
from www.millsandboon.co.uk**

CHAPTER ONE

THICK grass spiked at Tessa King's bare knees as she sank to the ground beside the tiny, immaculately kept grave. Large trees shaded the cemetery and birdsong was the only noise that broke the drowsy afternoon serenity as she laid the bright yellow daffodils near the miniature marble statue of a kneeling angel.

Grief bloomed in her chest, sharp and fresh, rising in her throat, threatening to choke her. She squeezed her eyes shut and sucked in a breath, reaching for the headstone as the tsunamilike wave of emotion unbalanced her.

She let some tears escape. Just a few.

No more.

Even on the anniversary of his death she rationed her grief. It was ten years to the day since Ryan had died. Ten years of living life in greyscale.

The memories struggled for release but not even on this day did she allow herself the luxury of remembering too much. She rationed the memories too. His little body squirming against hers, his boyish giggle and that perfect little bow mouth.

The double cowlick that had refused to be tamed.

It was enough.

Tess opened her eyes, the simple inscription she

knew as intimately as she knew her own heartbeat, blurring in front of her.

Ryan King.
Aged 18 months.
Gone, and a cloud in our hearts.

She reached for the letters, the smooth marble cool beneath her fingertips. She didn't let them linger. She wiped at her cheeks, blinked the remaining moisture away.

Enough.

Fletcher King ground his heels into the luxurious carpet of grass, resisting the urge to go to her as she sagged against the headstone. His butt stayed stubbornly planted against the bonnet of his Jag. She'd made it perfectly clear when they'd separated that it had to be a clean break. That she didn't want to see him or talk to him, and every overture he'd made the first year to keep in touch, to check on her, had been resoundingly rebuffed.

Frankly, after nine years of watching this ritual from afar, he didn't even know how to approach her. She seemed as distant today as she had for that awful year after Ryan's death when their marriage had slowly shrivelled and died.

He hadn't been able to bridge the gap back then and he doubted almost a decade of distance would have improved things.

It didn't mean he was immune to her grief. Even from this distance the weight of her despair punched him square in the solar plexus. Took him right back to the dreadful day as they'd frantically tried to revive their son, hoping against hope, trying to ignore the portent of doom that had settled over him like a leaden cloak.

His frantic *'Come on, Ryan, come on*!' still echoed in his dreams all these years later.

A lump rose in his throat, tears needled and stung his eyes and he squeezed them tightly shut. He'd already cried a river or two; hell, he was probably up to an ocean by now, but he couldn't afford to succumb today.

He was here on a mission.

He needed his wife back.

Tess put one foot in front of the other on autopilot as she made her way to her car. Whether it was because of the dark swirl of emotions or the jet-lag, she didn't see him or at least register the identity of the tall, broad man leaning against the car parked in front of her rental until she was two metres away.

Then, as her belly did that almost forgotten somersault and her breath hitched in the same way it used to, she wondered why the hell not. She may not have been interested in a man in ten years but she obviously wasn't totally dead inside.

And Fletcher King in dark trousers and a business shirt that had been rolled up to the elbows and undone at the throat was still an incredibly impressive man.

In fact, if anything, the years had honed him into an even more spectacular specimen.

He looked broader across the shoulders. Leaner at the hips. There were streaks of grey at his temples and where his dark, wavy hair met sculpted cheekbones. His three-day growth, black as midnight last time she'd seen it, was lightly peppered with salt. There were interesting lines around his tired-looking eyes, which were the silvery-green colour of wattle leaves.

Did he, too, still have trouble sleeping?

The indentations around his mouth, which became dimples when he laughed, were deeper. Even his mouth seemed fuller—sexier. His lips parted slightly and she caught a glimpse of his still-perfect teeth.

'Hello, Tessa.'

Tess was surprised by the prickle of awareness as his soft voice rumbled across the void between them. The latent attraction was unexpected. She was so used to locking down anything that had an emotional impact on her she was amazed she could still feel a pull at all.

But this *was* Fletch.

'Fletcher.' So much lay unsaid between them she didn't know where to start. 'It's been a long time.'

Fletch nodded, stifled by their formality. 'How have you been?'

She shrugged. 'Fine.'

Fletch suppressed a snort. *Hardly.* Each year she seemed to have faded away a little more. Gone were those curves that had driven him to distraction. There were only angles now. The legs sticking out of her above-knee, cargo-style pants were slender, her collar bones visible through the V-opening of her modest T-shirt were like coat hangers.

'You've got very thin.'

She shrugged again. 'Yes.' Tess ate as a matter of survival. Her pleasure in it had been sucked away with all the other things that had once brought her joy.

He regarded her for a moment. She was still a striking woman despite the angles. And the uber-short hairstyle. She'd cut it some time in that first year after they'd separated. She'd once had long white-blonde hair that had flowed down her back and formed a perfect curtain around them when they'd been making love. He'd spent hours stroking it, wrapping it around his hands and watching the light turn it incandescent as it had slowly sifted through his fingers.

It was darker blonde now, more honey than snow—a direct consequence of moving far away from the sunshine of Brisbane to the drizzly English countryside. It was cropped closely to her head, the back and sides razored severely in. The slightly longer locks on top were brushed over from a side parting, blending in with the jagged edges.

His sister had called it minimalist. He'd preferred the term butchered.

It did, however, draw attention to her amber eyes. They sat large in her spare, make-up-less face, dominating prominent cheekbones that fell away to catwalk-model hollows. They looked at him now, shadows playing in their sherry depths.

Her composure reached across the space between them and squeezed his gut hard. She projected calm detachment but he knew her well enough, despite their time apart, to see beyond. There was a fragility about her he'd have not thought possible a decade ago.

The impact of it rattled the shackles around his heart.

Tess weathered his probing gaze, waiting for him to say something more. Finally she could bear the silence no longer. She cleared her throat. 'I have to go.'

Fletch's gaze was drawn to her mouth. Her wide, full lips were devoid of any cosmetic enhancement, just as he remembered them. The same mouth he must have kissed a thousand times. That had travelled over every inch of his body. The same mouth that had desperately tried to breathe life into Ryan, that had begged a God she'd never believed in to spare their son.

Tess took a step towards her car. 'I have to go,' she repeated.

Fletch blocked her path, gently snagging her wrist. 'Could we talk?'

Tessa recoiled from his hold as if she'd been zapped, crossing her arms across her chest. 'There's nothing to talk about.'

'It's been nine years, Tess. You think we have nothing to say to each other?'

Tess bit her lip. *Nothing that hadn't been said already—ad nauseam.*

Fletch glanced at her white-knuckled grip as her fingernails dug into the flesh of her bare biceps. Her wedding ring, *his grandmother's ring*, snagged his attention. 'You still wear your wedding ring.'

Tess, surprised by the sudden direction the conversation had taken, looked down at it. The rose-gold band with its engraved floral pattern, thinned with age and wear, hung loosely on her finger, only her knuckle preventing it from sliding off. She absently twisted it around with her thumb a few times before returning her attention to him.

'Yes.' She wasn't going to tell him it was her deterrent against unwanted advances from men. She glanced at his bare left hand. 'You don't.'

Fletcher glanced at his hand. It had taken a year after the divorce to take it off yet sometimes he was still surprised by its absence. The white tan line that had remained after he'd removed it had long since faded.

'No.' It had got to the stage where he hadn't been able to bear the memories it had evoked.

Tess nodded. What had she expected? That he would

choose to hide behind his as she had hers? That grief would torpedo his libido as it had hers?

Tess dropped her arms to her sides. 'I really have to go.'

Fletch held up his hands. 'I just need a minute, please.'

She felt exasperation bubble in her chest. In less than twenty-four hours she'd be back on a plane heading to London. The same as last year. The same as the last nine years. Why had he chosen to complicate things now?

'What do you want, Fletch?' What could he possibly want to say to her after all this time? After all these years of silence? Silence they'd *both* agreed on despite his lapses early in their separation.

Fletch blinked as her familiar name for him finally slipped from her lips to claw at his gut. 'It's my mother...she's unwell. She's been asking for you.'

Tess felt her stomach drop as concern for her ex-mother-in-law caused her heart to leap in her chest. Fletch looked so grim. 'Is she...? What's wrong with her? What happened?'

'She has Alzheimer's.'

Tessa gasped, her hand coming up to cover her mouth. 'Oh, Fletch...' She took a step towards him, their baggage momentarily forgotten, her other hand reaching for him.

'That's terrible.' Her hand settled against his arm, her fingers on the sleeve of his business shirt, her palm against the corded muscles of his tanned forearm. 'Is it... Is she bad?'

Jean King was one of the sharpest women Tess had ever met. She was funny, witty, insightful and super-smart. Tess's mother had died when she'd been eight and Jean had filled a very deep void. They'd been close

right from the get-go and Jean had been her anchor—
their anchor—in the dreadful months that had followed
Ryan's death. Even when she and Fletch had separated
and then divorced, Jean had been there for her.

Fletch nodded. 'She's deteriorated in the last couple
of months.'

'When… How long has she had it for?'

Tess had dropped in on Jean on her yearly pilgrimage home those first two years after she'd moved to the
UK. But it had been too hard on both of them. Jean had
wanted to talk about Ryan and Tess hadn't been able to
bear it. So she'd stopped going.

Fletch, aware of her nearness, of her faint passionfruit fragrance, of her hand on his arm, waged a war
within himself. Tess looked as devastated as he felt and
it was as if the intervening years had never happened.
As if he could walk right into her arms and seek the
solace he so desperately craved.

It was a dangerous illusion.

He couldn't hope to execute what he'd come here for
if he let emotion take over. He just hadn't been prepared
for how hard it would be, seeing her again, talking to
her again. He'd foolishly thought it would be easy.

Well…easier.

He gave himself a mental shake and rubbed the back
of his neck. 'She was first diagnosed five years ago.
She's been living with Trish for the last two years.'

'Five years?' she gasped. Tess couldn't even begin
to comprehend a world where Jean King was anything
less than her larger-than-life self. 'Why…why didn't
you tell me?'

Fletch raised an eyebrow. 'Seriously, Tess? I rang
you practically every day for a year after you went to

England.… You made it pretty clear that no correspondence would be entered into. Anyway, what were you going to do?' he asked, surprised at the bitterness in his tone. 'Come home?'

Tess bit her lip. He was right. She had been ruthless with her no-contact request. 'I'm sorry…'

She searched his silvery-green gaze and saw apprehension and worry and for one crazy moment almost took another step forward to embrace him. But a decade of denial slammed the door shut and she dropped her hand from his arm, shocked at the strength of the impulse.

She shook her head. 'It's just so wrong. Your mum has always been as fit as a fiddle…'

Fletch felt her withdrawal from their intimacy as keenly as if it had been ten years ago.

Damn it.

Did she really think because she hadn't moved on that things weren't going to change around her? 'She's seventy-four, Tess. She's getting old. Did you think she was just always going to be here, frozen in time, waiting for you to come around?'

Tess recoiled as if he had slapped her, colour draining from her face. 'I doubt your mother has been sitting around waiting on me,' she retaliated.

'You're like a second daughter to her, Tess,' he dismissed impatiently. 'She's missed you every day.'

I've missed you every day.

Fletch blinked at the thought. *He had.* Standing here in front of her, talking to her for the first time in nine years, he realised just how deeply he had missed her.

Tess felt the truth of his starkly delivered words wrap around her heart and squeeze. She wanted to deny them but she couldn't. He was right. They had been close. And Jean *was* getting older.

Fletch sighed as Tess gnawed on her bottom lip, looking utterly wretched. He raised his hands in a half-surrender.

'I'm sorry, I didn't mean to...' To what? Get angry with her? Make her feel guilty? 'Will you, please, just come and see her? She gets anxious easily these days and you're the one she wants to see the most.'

Tess was torn. She'd love to see Jean again. Had missed her wise counsel and warm hugs over the years. And if it helped ease some of her mother-in-law's anxiety to see her then that was the least Tess could do. But would it be Jean? And would it build an expectation, make it harder to walk away?

Because she was getting on that plane tomorrow. Just like she did every year.

And most importantly, what if Jean wanted to talk about Ryan? What if she didn't remember he was dead? Talked about him as if he was alive and just down for a nap?

Tess looked at Fletcher. 'What about...?' She cleared her throat as a lump formed there. Even just saying it was beyond difficult. 'What does she remember from...?'

Fletcher watched the shimmer of emotion in Tess's amber gaze as she struggled with her words. He shook his head. 'She doesn't remember him at all, Tess.'

It had been a particularly difficult thing for Fletch to cope with. After Tess had refused to hear his name, his mother had been the only person he'd been able to talk openly with about Ryan.

Now it was as if his son had never existed.

'Her memory seems to stretch to about a year after we were married. As far as she's concerned, we've just got back from Bora Bora.'

Fletch had taken Tess to the tropical paradise for a surprise first wedding anniversary present. They'd lazed in their over-water bungalow all day. Making love, drinking cocktails and watching the multitude of colourful fish swim by their glass floor.

He shrugged. 'There's an occasional recall of an event beyond that but it's rare.'

For a brief moment Tess envied Jean. The thought of forgetting how Ryan had felt in her arms or at her breast, forgetting the way his hair had stuck up in the middle from his double cowlick and how his giggle had filled the whole room. Forgetting that gut-wrenching day and all the empty days that had followed since.

It sounded like bliss.

The fantasy was shocking, wrong on so many levels, and she quickly moved to erase it from her mind. Jean was suffering from a debilitating disease that was ravaging her brain and would rob her of her most basic functions.

There was no upside to that.

And no justice in this world.

Although she already knew that more intimately than most.

Tess nodded. 'Okay.'

Fletch blinked at her easy capitulation. 'Really?'

'Sure.' She frowned, his disbelief irksome. 'For Jean.' He should know she'd do anything for his mother. 'Did you think I wouldn't?'

He shrugged. 'Yes.'

His bluntness hurt but she pushed it aside—it was,

after all, a fair statement. She *had* been sneaking into the country once a year for the last nine years with only two paltry visits to Jean to defend herself against his conviction.

But they'd agreed on a clean break.

And she'd stuck to it.

Eventually, so had he.

She gave him a measured look. 'It's Jean.'

Fletch nodded as the husky note in her voice didn't mask her meaning. She wasn't doing it for him.

And that was certainly what he was counting on now.

'Thank you.' He gestured to his car. 'Do you want to follow me?'

Tess shook her head. 'She's at Trish's, right? They still live in Indooroopilly?'

Fletch shook his head. 'No, she's at my place for the moment.'

Tess blinked. 'You have a place in Brisbane?'

Since their separation Fletch had moved to Canada, where he'd been heavily involved in research and travelling the world lecturing. Or at least the last time she'd heard, that had been where he'd been. It was suddenly weird having absolutely no idea where he lived—or any of the details of his life for the last nine years.

She honestly hadn't cared until today but it somehow seemed wrong now to know so little about someone whose life had been so closely entwined with hers for so long they may as well have been conjoined.

When she thought about him, which she still did with uncomfortable regularity, it was always against the backdrop of their marital home. The ninety-year-old worker's cottage they'd renovated together.

Polished the floorboards, painted the walls, built the pergola.

The house they'd brought Ryan home to as a new-born.

'I'm renting an apartment on the river.'

'Oh. Okay.'

Tess tamped down on her surprise. Fletch had always despised apartment living. Had loved the freedom of large living spaces and a back yard.

But, then, a lot of things had changed over the last ten years.

'Right,' she said. 'I'll follow you.'

Fletch nodded. 'It's only about a ten-minute drive. See you soon.'

'Sure,' Tess murmured, then walked on shaky legs to her car.

Nine minutes later they drove into the underground car park of a swanky apartment block. She pulled her cheap hire car in beside his Jag in his guest car space. They didn't talk as he ushered her to the lifts or while they waited for one to arrive.

Tess stared at the floor, the doors, the ugly concrete walls of the chilly underground car park—what did one say, how did one act around one's ex? An ex she'd deliberately put at a fifteen-thousand-kilometre distance?

A lift arrived, promptly derailing her line of thought. He indicated for her to precede him, which she did, and then stood back as Fletch pushed the button for the nineteenth floor. More silence followed. Surely at least they could indulge in inane conversation for the duration of their time together?

A sudden thought occurred to her and she looked at him leaning against the opposite wall. 'How did you know I was going to be there today?'

Fletch returned her look. 'Because you're there every year on the anniversary.'

Tess blinked at his calm steady gaze. 'How do you know that?'

'Because I watch you.'

Another silence descended between them as her brain tried to compute what he'd just said. 'You *watch* me?'

He nodded. 'Nine years ago you were leaving as I was arriving.' He remembered how close he'd come to calling her name. 'I thought you might come back the next year. You did. And the year after that. So now I... wait for you.'

The lift dinged. The doors opened. Neither of them moved. The doors started to close and Fletch shot an arm out to push them open again. 'After you,' he murmured.

Tess couldn't move for a moment. She stared at him. 'Why?'

'I know you think that your grief is deeper than mine but he was my son too, Tess. I also like to visit on the anniversary.'

Tessa flinched at the bitterness in his voice. And then again when the lift doors started beeping, protesting their prolonged open state. She walked out, dazed, conscious of Fletch slipping past her, leading the way down a long plush hallway with trendy inkspot carpeting. She followed slowly, still trying to get her head around Fletch's revelation.

She drew level with him, glancing up from the floor. 'I meant why wait for me? Why not just visit for a while and leave?'

Like she did.

Fletch wished he knew the answer to that question. It was the same thing he told himself every year as he set out for the cemetery. Go, talk with Ryan for a bit, then leave.

But he didn't. He'd sit in his car and wait for her. Watch her kneel beside Ryan's grave.

Torture himself just a little bit more.

He shrugged. 'To see you.'

CHAPTER TWO

'Mum, we're home,' Fletch called as he opened the door, checking behind him to see if Tess was following or still standing in the hallway like a stunned mullet.

He wasn't sure why he'd said what he'd said. Except it was the truth. He just hadn't realised it until right that moment. He'd kidded himself that it was to check up on her but now he knew it was more.

That there was part of him, no matter how hard he'd tried to move on, that just hadn't.

He walked into the apartment, throwing his keys on the hallstand. 'Mother?'

A voice came from the direction of the bathroom. 'I'm in here, darling, there's no need to shout.' Jean appeared a moment later with a spray pack in one hand and a mop in the other.

'Mum, you don't have to clean the apartment,' Fletch said, trying to keep the exasperation and relief out of his voice as he unburdened her of her load.

He didn't like to leave his mother alone for too long these days. She seemed so frail and unsteady on her feet and he worried she might fall and injure herself while he was out.

Especially if she was mopping floors.

'I have a cleaning lady for that.'

'Nonsense, darling, I have to make myself useful somehow. Now, is Tess working late or shall I put something on for tea for her tonight?'

Tess stepped out of the shadow of the entranceway where she'd been frozen since Jean had entered the room. Jean, who had once been a towering Amazon of a woman and was now white-haired and stooped and looked like a puff of wind would blow her over.

She sucked in a breath at the absurd urge to cry. 'No, Jean, I'm here.'

Jean looked over her son's shoulder and smiled. 'Oh, Tess! There you are!' She hurried forward and pulled Tess into an effusive hug. 'Goodness, you're getting so skinny,' Jean tutted, pulling back to look at her daughter-in-law. 'And your hair! Did you have that done today? I love it!'

Tess swallowed hard at the shimmer of moisture in Jean's eyes as her mother-in-law wrapped her in another hug. She shut her eyes as she was sucked into a bizarre time warp where the last decade and all its horrible events just didn't exist. She held tight to Jean's bony shoulders.

Her mother-in-law had become an old woman while she'd been away. Guilt clawed at her.

'How about a cuppa?' Jean said, finally letting Tess go.

'Great idea, Mum,' Fletch agreed. 'Why don't you take Tess through and I'll get the tea?'

Jean smiled and nodded. She turned to go then stopped, her smile dying as a look of confusion clouded her gaze. She looked at her son blankly.

'Over there,' Fletch murmured gently as he pointed to the corner of the open-plan living space where a leather three-piece suite, a coffee table and a large-screen television formed a lounge area.

Jean's gaze followed the direction of Fletch's finger. It took a moment or two for the set-up to register. 'Of course.' She shook her head. 'Come on, Tess. Tell me all about work today.'

Tess moved off with Jean but not before her gaze locked with Fletch's. She saw his despair and felt an answering flicker. No wonder Fletch had looked tired earlier—this had to be killing him.

Jean patted the cushion beside her and asked, 'How was the unit today, dear? Busy as usual?'

Tess sat beside Jean, bringing her thoughts back to order. 'I…' She glanced at Fletch for direction.

Since moving to England Tess had changed her speciality to geriatrics so nursing Alzheimer's patients was part and parcel of what she did every day. But each patient was individual and responded differently to having their misstatements corrected.

He nodded his head encouragingly, which didn't really tell her very much. 'I didn't go to work today,' she sidestepped. 'It was my day off and I had…some business to attend to.'

'Ah, well, no doubt Fletch will know. Fletch?'

'It wasn't too bad, Mum,' Fletch said as he placed a tray with three steaming mugs on the coffee table and apportioned them. He sat on the nearby single-seater. 'Still a lot of kids with the last of the winter bugs getting themselves into a pickle.'

Tess picked up her mug and absently blew on it. So they were validating Jean's false sense of reality? At this stage of her disease it was probably all that was left to do. Too many dementia patients became confused and distressed when confronted with their memory loss, and to what end? They were too far gone to realise what was happening to them.

Jean sighed and looked from one to the other. 'I'm so proud of both of you. It can't be easy going to work each day looking after such sick little kiddies.'

Tess squeezed Jean's hand in response. What else could she do? She and Fletch hadn't worked at St Rita's Paediatric Intensive Care Unit together for ten years. Not since Ryan had died there. In fact, she hadn't been able to return to that field of practice at all, hence her move to the other end of the spectrum altogether.

Fletch changed the subject to the weather and they let Jean lead from there, navigating a maze of patch-work conversation—some lucid, some not so lucid. They got on to the spectacular view from the floor-to-ceiling glass doors, with Jean teasing Fletch about his fancy apartment. 'I can't believe you two got this thing. What happened to that gorgeous little cottage you were renovating?'

Fletch smiled at his mother. 'We sold it. Too much hard work.'

'Oh, pish,' Jean said, swatting her hand through the air. 'As if you're afraid of hard work.'

Tess swallowed a lump as Jean, despite the demen-tia, looked at her son the way she always had, like he could hang the moon. Fletch's father had died when he and his sister, Trish, had both been very young and Fletch had been the man of the house for a long time.

'Gosh, Tess,' Jean remarked, shaking her head. 'Look how skinny you are! And where did that lovely tan go? I can't believe how quickly that gorgeous tan of yours has faded. It hasn't been that long since you've been back from Bora Bora.'

Fletch felt the bleakness inside ratchet up another notch. *The tan had gone to England and never come back!*

Jean held up an imperious finger. 'Hold on a moment.' And she scurried off towards the direction she'd originally come from.

Tess felt exhausted with jet-lag and trying to keep up with Jean's meandering conversation and rapid-fire subject changes. But not as exhausted as Fletch looked. 'What medication is she on?' she asked.

Fletch rattled off a series of the most up-to-date dementia pills on the market. He shrugged. 'They've held it at bay for many years but—'

Jean bustled back in, interrupting them. 'Here it is,' she said, brandishing a book of some description. When she sat down and opened it Tess realised it was a photo album. The one she'd put together all those years ago after their return from Bora Bora.

Fletch frowned as a hundred memories flooded his mind. He shook his head slightly at Tess's questioning look. He'd had no idea his mother had this album. It, along with all the others, had been stored in one of the many boxes that he'd packed their marriage into after he and Tess had separated and she'd run away to the other side of the world.

Maybe when he'd asked his mother to get rid of it all just prior to his move to Canada, she'd decided to keep a few souvenirs? He hadn't really cared at the time how she'd made it disappear, just that it had. God knew, he hadn't been able to bear the thought of going through it all himself, deciding what to keep and what to discard.

Getting rid of it all, holus bolus, had been a much easier option.

And yet here was a part of it, turning up like the proverbial bad penny. A full Technicolor reminder of how happy they'd been.

'See, now look at you here,' Jean said, pointing to Tess in a bikini on the beach. 'Brown as a berry!'

Tessa stared at the photograph, shocked by the sudden yank back into the past. She'd taken three photos from the ruins of their marriage—all of Ryan. Not that she'd been able to bear to look at them. They lived at the back of a cupboard she never opened.

But it had been a long time since she'd seen ones of Fletch and herself.

A stranger stared back at her. Yes, she *was* very tanned. She was also deliriously happy, obviously in love and blissfully unaware of the giant black hole hovering in her future. In fact, the woman in the photograph looked nothing like the woman she was today.

And it had nothing to do with the tan.

For a fleeting second, Tess wished she could jump into the photo, like Mary Poppins had jumped into that pavement painting, and give herself a good shake.

If only she'd known then what she knew now.

If only...

'I think this is my favourite one,' Jean said, flipping to one of Fletch, towel wrapped around his waist, elbows on the balcony railing, looking back over his shoulder and laughing into the camera, crystal waters behind him.

Tessa stilled as she remembered she'd been fresh from the shower and naked when she'd taken that picture and the series of intimate photos that had followed—ones that had not made it into this album! She remembered making him lie on the bed and loosen his towel, snapping shots of every glorious inch of his body.

Then he'd grappled the camera from her and returned

the favour, asking her to pose for him and taking a set of photos a professional photographer would have been proud of. To this day the one on her stomach, looking over her shoulder with her hair flowing down her back, the sheet ruched around her bottom revealing only the slight rise of one cheek, was the best picture ever taken of her.

She remembered being so turned on by their nude photo session they'd made love for hours afterwards, rolling and sighing and moaning to the gentle swish of the waves.

She glanced at Fletch—did he remember?

His gaze locked with hers, turning almost silver as heat flashed like a solar flare. It dropped to her mouth and she watched as his throat bobbed.

'It's my favourite too,' Fletch murmured.

Oh, yeah, he remembered.

Tess sat through the rest of the album, desperately trying to claw back some control of her brain. Bora Bora was in the past—a long time in the past. She hadn't come here to take a walk down memory lane, although she guessed to a degree that had been inevitable. Neither had she come to rekindle the sexual attraction that, prior to Ryan's death, had always raged like an inferno between them.

She'd come for Jean. To alleviate some anxiety and then turn around and go back to her perfectly fulfilling, asexual, far-away existence.

Jean closed the album. 'I think you two need to go back to Bora Bora. You're both too tense.' She patted Tess's hand. 'And pale.'

Before Tess could answer, an alarm blared out and she jumped slightly at the same time Jean clutched at her chest and looked at Fletch anxiously.

'It's okay, Mum,' Fletch reassured her as he reached over and turned off the alarm on the clock that was sitting on the coffee table. 'Remember, that just means your show's about to start.' His mother continued to look at him blankly. 'Wheel of Fortune,' he prompted.

'Oh.' Jean sagged a little and dropped her hand to her lap. 'Oh, yes, oh, I love that show!'

Fletch nodded as he picked up the remote and flicked on the big sleek screen to the channel that played non-stop 1980s television shows. 'There you go, just starting,' he said as the game-show music rang out.

'Tess.' Jean bounced like a little girl on Christmas morning. 'Do you want to watch it with me?'

Fletch watched the play of emotions mirrored in Tess's eyes. She was obviously shocked by the many faces of Jean. 'Actually, we're going to go out on to the deck and have a chat,' he said.

But his mother wasn't listening, engrossed in the show, her invitation to Tess already forgotten. He inclined his head at Tess, indicating they move away, and she eagerly complied, following him to the kitchen.

'Would you like something a little stronger?' he asked as he removed the mug she'd brought with her and placed it in the sink.

Following a period after she'd moved to the UK when she'd drunk a little too often, Tessa didn't drink much these days. But if ever she needed alcohol, it was now. Being with Jean was heartbreaking. And being with Fletch, seeing those pictures, was…disturbing.

'Yes, please.'

Fletch pulled a bottle of chilled white wine out of the fridge and held it up. 'All right?'

Tessa nodded. 'Sure. Thanks.'

He poured them both a glass and handed her hers.

Normally he'd clink glasses with someone in this situation but nothing was normal about right now so he took a mouthful then led the way to the deck.

Fletch, conscious of her behind him, put his arms on the railing and inhaled the late-afternoon river breeze. He took another sip of his wine then turned to face her.

'Thank you,' he said.

'I'm so sorry, Fletch,' she murmured. 'It's…it's so unfair.'

Fletch's lips twisted into a bitter smile as his mobile phone rang. 'Since when has life ever been fair?' he asked as he located his phone and answered it.

Tess nodded. *Truer words had never been spoken.*

She moved to the far side of the railing to give Fletch some privacy. She had absolutely no desire to eavesdrop on the conversation but it was hard not to when he was standing two metres from her.

It was Trish and Tess gathered Fletch's little sister was asking after Jean. Then she heard Fletch tell her that he'd been to the cemetery and reassured her three times that he was fine. Like Jean, Trish had been a tremendous support for them after losing Ryan. She'd worried about them, about her brother particularly, like a little mother hen. Tess knew that if Trish had been able to turn back time for them, she would have.

Her name was mentioned and Tess wondered how Trish was taking the news that she was here. They'd been close once, like real sisters, but Trish was loyal to a fault and while she'd been supportive for that horrible year, she'd been angry with Tess over her desertion of Fletch.

It had hurt at the time but blood was thicker than water and it was only right that she should stand by her brother.

Fletch hung up. 'Sorry, that was Trish.'

'So I gathered,' she murmured, swishing the wine in her glass absently. 'How's she and Doug doing these days?'

'Great. Doug started his own computer repair business five years ago. It's thriving. Trish gave up the child-care centre a few years ago to work full time taking care of the books side of things and managing the job schedule. They have Christopher, he's almost two. And she's seven months pregnant with number two.'

Tess stilled, the swirl of the wine coming to a halt. She glanced at Fletch. Trish had a child? A little boy. A little boy only a few months older than Ryan had been when he'd died?

And another on the way?

She and Fletch had been trying for another baby just prior to Ryan's accident.

The ache that was never far from her heart intensified. In a split second she both envied and despised her ex-sister-in-law with shocking intensity.

Fletch watched Tess's face as a string of emotions chased across the taut face, which seemed suddenly paler. 'She always wanted babies, Tess,' he said gently.

Tess breathed in raggedly. She nodded her head vigorously. 'Of course.' Trish had absolutely doted on Ryan. 'That's great,' she said, forcing words past the husky lump lodged in her larynx. 'So, you're an uncle, huh?'

Fletch nodded. 'Yes.'

Of sorts. He hadn't had a lot to do with his nephew given how often he was out of the country. But he was a dear little boy who adored him. And if it was hard at times to hold his wriggly little body and not think of Ryan, not see the similarities between the two cousins, then he erected another layer around his heart and sucked it up.

Tess heard the grimness in his response and knew that it couldn't have been easy for him. She hesitated for a moment, went to take a step towards him until a shout of 'Buy a vowel!' coming from the lounge area halted the reflex before her foot had even moved.

She smiled at him as the sound of Jean's excited clapping drifted out. 'How's Jean with him?'

Fletch felt his answering smile die. 'She doesn't remember him most days. It's hard for Trish. Especially as Mum's been living with them since just before Christopher was born.'

Tess frowned. 'How come she's living with you now? I don't mean to tell you how to manage Jean's condition but I don't think changing her living arrangements at this stage in her disease is such a good thing, Fletch.'

'Trish had problems with her first pregnancy. She went into early labour at twenty-four weeks. They managed to stop it and get the pregnancy through to thirty-four weeks. A month ago she went into early labour again with this one. Which they also managed to stop. But given her history and her age, her obstetrician ordered bed rest and no stress for the remainder of the pregnancy.'

'Ah,' Tess murmured. 'Not very easy when you're looking after a toddler and your high-needs mother.'

Fletch grimaced. 'No.' He rubbed the back of his neck. 'Trish tried day respite but the unfamiliar setting distressed Mum, made her anxious, which flowed on into the nights. Mum stopped sleeping and she started to wander. She had a couple of falls.'

'Oh, no,' Tess gasped.

Fletch shrugged. 'Lucky she has bones made of concrete.'

Tess laughed, remembering the time that Jean had slipped and fallen down a flight of stairs with not even a bruise to show for it. Fletch smiled at her laugh. It was as familiar to him as his own and yet not something he'd heard for a very long time.

Another thing he'd missed with surprising ferocity.

'We got a day nurse in but the same thing happened. An unfamiliar face just aggravated the situation. So...I took a leave of absence from Calgary and came home to step in and do my bit. Look after Mum until after the baby's born.'

Tess understood the conundrum he and Trish faced. The familiar was important to dementia patients, who clung to their repertoire of the familiar even as it shrank at an alarming rate around them. But, still, uprooting yourself from the other side of the world was a big ask.

Although she guessed not for Fletch. He'd always been very family orientated, always taken care of his responsibilities.

'It's a good thing you're doing,' she said softly.

He looked at her. 'It's family, Tess. Family sticks together.'

Tess shied from the intensity of his silver-green eyes. Was there an accusation there? Sure, she'd asked for the divorce but he hadn't exactly put up a fight. In fact, he'd been pretty relieved as far as she could recall. Did he really blame her for wanting to get as far away from it all as possible?

She took a deep breath. She wasn't going to go there. She was finishing her drink. She was going back to her hotel room.

Tomorrow she was getting on a plane.

'So you're not working, then?'

Fletch shook his head. He looked into his drink. 'That was the plan but St Rita's approached me with an interesting proposition and I've accepted a temporary contract...'

Tess blinked as the information sat like a lead sinker in her brain. 'St Rita's? In the...PICU?'

Fletch glanced up into her huge amber eyes, flashing their incredulity like a lighthouse beacon. 'In both the adult and kids' ICUs. They want someone to head up a study on the application of hypothermia in acute brain injury. They've asked me. I didn't come here to work but...how could I refuse? It's a marvellous opportunity.'

Tess was quiet for a moment while she processed the startling information. 'Oh.'

She knew that since their separation and his move to Canada, Fletch had become an authority—*some might call it an obsession*—on cold-water drowning, undertaking several world-renowned studies. In fact, he was probably one of the world's foremost experts on the subject. She'd read everything he'd ever published from the impressive studies to journal articles and every paper he'd ever given at a conference or a symposium.

None of them had brought Ryan back.

'It's part time, only a few hours a day with no real clinical role. I can do a lot of the work from home, which is perfect, leaves me a lot of time for Mum.'

Tess nodded. It sounded ideal. She just wished she could understand how he could go back there. She knew, although she didn't pretend to comprehend, why he'd chosen that particular field of research but how he could handle the subject matter was beyond her. And how he could enter St Rita's without breaking down she'd never know.

Her eyes sought his. She remembered how he'd told his mother earlier about the kids with the last of the winter bugs. She'd thought he'd been fobbing Jean off but obviously not. 'You've…you've been into the PICU?'

Their gazes locked. 'Yes. Several times. In fact, I called in there on my way to the cemetery.'

Tess let out a shaky breath. 'Right…'

What did she say now? How was it? Have you been into room two? Did it bring back memories? Was Ryan's presence still there or had it been erased by years of other children and hospital antiseptic?

Instead, she said nothing because she really didn't want to know.

Fletch's stare didn't waver. 'It wasn't easy, Tess.'

She looked away. *Had he thought it would be?* Did he expect her sympathy? An embrace? Applause? Some kind of a shared moment where everything was suddenly all right because he'd confronted some ghosts?

A surge of emotions knotted in her belly and she knew she had to leave. Get out. Far away from Fletch and all that reminded her of that dark, dark time.

Denial had been working for her just fine.

She just wanted to go to bed and sleep off the jet-lag and not have to think about any of it.

'Well,' she said, downing the contents of her glass in one long swallow. 'It looks like you have everything worked out.'

'Tess.'

She ignored the reproach in his voice. 'I've gotta go.' She placed the wine glass on the table and headed for the door.

'Tess,' he said, catching her arm lightly as she brushed past him.

Tess stopped. 'Let me go,' she said, staring straight ahead.

'Tess, please, stay for a while.'

She squeezed her eyes shut. 'Fletch.'

'I want to talk to you, Tess.'

'I think we're all talked out.'

'It's about Mum.' He felt her arm strain against his hand. 'Please, Tess, just hear me out. For Jean.'

Tess sighed, and her muscles relaxed, knowing she was defeated.

Damn it.

And damn him.

CHAPTER THREE

TESS sat at the table, staring out over the Brisbane River, while Fletch was in the kitchen fixing them both a top-up of their glasses. A light breeze ruffled her utilitarian locks and she had to shake herself to believe she was actually sitting on her ex-husband's deck, drinking wine.

The whole scene felt surreal. Jean's dementia had dragged her reluctantly into her past. A time when things had been simple and she'd truly believed that love could get a person through everything. It was a strange reality that warred with her present-day situation.

What did he want to talk to her about regarding Jean? Surely he had better access to the medical side of Jean's condition than she did? He probably had half a dozen gerontologists up his sleeve he could talk to. Or maybe he was after practical advice? How to care for his mother on a day-to-day basis? Or a recommendation for a good home-care agency, maybe?

Whatever it was, she hoped he made it snappy because when she got to the bottom of her second glass she was walking away.

Fletch paused by the sliding door, watching Tess's profile for a moment, and wished he was sure of her. He needed her help. Once upon a time he could have counted on it. But a lot of water had flowed under the bridge since then and she was so very, very skittish.

Plus he wasn't so sure of himself now. His plan had sounded fine in theory but being with her again was confrontational on many levels. He'd thought he could handle it but standing two metres from her he realised it would be physically and emotionally harder than he'd ever imagined.

Still…he was desperate and Tess was perfect.

He took a deep breath and stepped out onto the deck. 'Here you go,' he said, placing her refilled wine glass in front of her.

Tess glanced down at the offering and murmured, 'Thanks.'

She picked it up and took a decent mouthful, the smooth, fruity crispness against her palate not really registering. She placed the wine back down as Fletch sat opposite her, hearing the clink as it met the smoky glass of the tabletop. 'You wanted to talk about Jean?' she prompted.

Fletch sighed. Obviously there wasn't going to be any small talk. Which he'd have preferred. He had no idea how she was going to react to his proposition, although instinct told him it wouldn't be very well…

'I need to get someone in for Mum. Someone who can be here while I'm out. When I accepted the contract I thought I'd be able to juggle it and her. It's only part time and Mum doesn't need constant care and attention. But the truth is I don't feel comfortable leaving her at all. I just don't think she's safe enough and I'd feel a hell of a lot better if she wasn't here by herself.'

'Like a home-care nurse?'

Fletch shook his head. 'No. I'm not after someone to help with her physical needs because she's still capable, so far, of taking care of that. Although having someone who understands Alzheimer's is a definite plus... I'm thinking more like a companion.'

'You mean someone closer to her own age?'

'I mean someone who knows her. She's not great with strangers—they distress her.'

Tess's brow wrinkled. 'That would be ideal, of course. Are you thinking of one of her old friends?'

Fletch didn't take his eyes off her. 'I'm thinking of someone closer than that. Someone she knows really well who has experience with the elderly and with dementia sufferers. The best of both worlds.'

Fletch watched and waited—waited for his meaning to sink in. It didn't take long.

Tess narrowed her eyes. Was Fletch thinking what she thought he was thinking? She shook her head at him. 'No. No way.'

'You're perfect, Tess.'

She shook her head again, mentally recoiling from the plea in his wattle-leaf gaze. 'No.'

'I know this is kind of out of the blue—'

'Kind of?' Tess spluttered.

'I wouldn't ask if I wasn't stuck.'

Tess stared at him, wondering when he was going to grow a second head. 'Putting *everything* else aside, I'm leaving for the UK tomorrow.'

'It's just until after Trish is back on her feet. A couple of months.'

Tess blinked. 'I have a *job,* Fletch.'

Fletch snorted. He'd always thought Tess squandering her critical care skills in a geriatric facility was such a monumental waste of a highly skilled nurse, even if it was to his advantage now.

She glared at him. 'That I love. Where I get an enormous amount of respect and job satisfaction.'

It might just be a little nursing-home in the middle of the Devonshire countryside but people depended on her. The staff and the residents. When she'd needed a place to hide and lick her wounds they'd taken her in and given her a direction for her life. They'd helped her function again.

'I'm sure they'd understand if you explained the circumstances. I can recompense you if it's money you're worried about.'

Tess shook her head at his utter gall. Had he thought she'd just agree? They'd been virtual strangers for the past nine years and he expected her to just...comply? And that splashing some money around would sweeten the pot? Sure, she loved Jean, he knew that. He knew how close they'd been. But it was still a big gamble for him to take—betting the bank on her.

The woman who had already turned her back on his family.

'So this is it?' she demanded. 'This is your brilliant plan? Ask your ex-wife? Who just happens to be here at the same time you need someone to look after your mother? That's crazy! What would you have done if I hadn't been in town?'

'It's not crazy. It makes absolute sense. You're the perfect person to ask. And, yes, the timing has been perfect too but, frankly, Tess, I would have gone to England to get you.'

'To *get* me?' Fletch held up his hands in a placatory manner.

'To ask you,' he amended.

Tess wasn't placated. 'How about this, Fletch? How about you give up *your* job and look after *your* mum instead? Trish's been doing it for two years. Surely you can take a lousy couple of months off to do your bit.'

Fletch nodded. 'And I will. If you won't…I will. But studies like this are so important, Tess. The results can help the way we treat acute head injury. What we learn from them can make a real difference to neurological outcomes. This is critical stuff, Tess.'

'Someone else can do it,' she snapped.

'Yes.' He nodded. 'Someone else could…but this is what I do.' He placed his hand on his chest. 'This is my field of expertise.' And his passion—Tess could hear it lacing every syllable. *But chasing after medical rainbows wasn't going to bring Ryan back.* She stood up, the metal chair legs scraping against the terracotta tiles.

'No, Fletcher. I'm sorry about your study, I really am, but I do not want to do this.'

He rose too and opened his mouth to interject and she held up a finger, silencing him. She looked into his determined face, his jaw set, his hand thrust on a hip, and she knew he didn't get it. Didn't understand why she'd be rejecting his perfectly rational plan.

He didn't understand how just being around them— him and Jean—would be like a hot knife to her chest every day. How the reminders of Ryan that she was able to keep rigorously at bay on the other side of the world would be torturous.

It was suddenly vitally important that he understand. Vitally.

'I get by, okay? I make it through each day and I sleep at night and my life is on an even keel. It may not seem very exciting to you—I'm not setting the world on fire with my cutting-edge research, but it took a while to reach this place and it works for me, Fletch. I don't want to undo it.'

Fletch felt his breath catch as the fierce glow of her amber eyes beseeched him. He held her gaze, ignoring the anguish he saw there. 'I came home the other day to a blaring alarm and smoke pouring out of the oven. She'd baked some biscuits and forgotten about them.'

He refused to look away, refused to back down. His mother was his priority and Tess was the answer. He needed her.

Whatever the emotional impact.

He was pushing her, he knew that, but listening to her talk had him thinking that maybe this was exactly what Tess needed also. Maybe she needed to start living a life where she more than just *got by.*

It was criminal that she was living this half-life stashed away in the English countryside where nobody knew her past and she could eke out an existence by pretending nothing had happened. That her whole world hadn't come crashing down and sucked her into the deepest, darkest despair.

Maybe it was time for both of them to confront the past and deal with it. To talk and grieve together instead of separately. He'd let her deny and avoid all those years ago because her sorrow had been all-consuming and he'd been walking through a minefield he'd had no idea how to navigate whilst suffering his own debilitating grief.

He hadn't pushed her back then.

But maybe it was finally time to push.

Tess swallowed as his intense look seemed to bore a hole right through her middle. It made her feel ill thinking about Jean almost burning the place down but her ex-mother-in-law wasn't her responsibility.

She was ex for a reason.

And she didn't want to get sucked back into lives

that were too closely entwined with the tragic events that had defined all their lives since.

It just would be too hard.

She shook her head and turned away. 'Goodbye, Fletcher.'

Fletch shut his eyes as she whirled away, heading for the door. *Damn it!* He'd felt sure he'd be able to convince her. He opened his eyes, resigned to letting it go. He'd tried. But he had to respect her decision.

Tess stalked into the apartment. *Wheel of Fortune* had finished, the show's theme song blaring out. Jean was nowhere to be seen.

'Jean?' Tess called, reaching for the remote. Nothing. Not that anything could be heard over the roar of the television. 'Jean?' she called again, hitting the mute button.

'Tess?'

Tess walked quickly towards the feeble, panicked voice she could hear coming from the kitchen area. 'Jean?'

'Here…I'm here.'

Tess rounded the bench to find Jean sitting on the floor, her back propped against the fridge, staring down at two raw eggs, one in each hand, the shells crushed, yolk oozing between her fingers. She looked at Tess with red-rimmed, frightened eyes, the papery skin on her cheeks damp.

'I don't know what these are,' she said to Tess, holding them up.

'Oh, Jean…' Tess sank to the floor beside her and put her arm around skinny shoulders. 'It's okay,' she murmured. 'It's going to be okay.'

Jean shook her head, pulled away to look at her daughter-in-law. 'I'm frightened, Tess,' she whispered, and started to tear up again. 'Something's wrong. H-help me, please.' Her voice cracked. 'Please…h-help me.'

Jean dissolved into soft tears and Tess felt her heart swell up with love for this woman who had been like a mother to her as she snuggled her into the crook of her shoulder.

'Shh,' Tess crooned, rocking slightly. 'Shh, now.'

Tess heard footsteps and looked up to find Fletch staring down at her with solemn eyes. He crouched beside them and Tess saw that all-too-familiar look of sadness sheen his eyes to silver. She watched as he reached for his mother's shoulder, placed his long brown fingers over her pale, waxy skin and gently rubbed.

'It's okay, Tess,' he whispered over his mother's bent head. 'I'll fix it.'

Tess shut her eyes as Jean's plea tugged at her. *She was almost out the door, damn it.* She didn't want to be needed like this. Not by Jean. And certainly not by him.

Not fair. So not fair.

But, as Fletch had only just pointed out, when had life ever been fair?

Could she really turn her back on Jean who had never asked her for anything? Fletch maybe, but Jean?

She opened her eyes. 'Let me see if it can be arranged…'

Fletch felt his heart swell with relief and something else far more primal. He sagged slightly as what seemed to be the weight of the entire world lifted from his shoulders. 'Thank you,' he mouthed. 'Thank you.'

Tess pushed the 'end' button on the phone thirty minutes later. Her boss at Estuary View Nursing Home had been very understanding of Tess's predicament and had urged Tess, her best employee who only ever took the same two weeks off every year, to take as much time as she needed.

So, that was that.

She kept her elbows firmly planted on the balcony railing, staring out over the river darkening to liquid mercury. The city's first lights winked on the polished surface and shimmered in the wake of a City Cat as it fractured the surface. She was surprised at the tide of nostalgia that crept over her.

Brisbane was her home town.

And she'd been away for a long time.

In recent years it had been a place to dread, a place of terrible memories, a heinous pilgrimage. But a sudden strange melancholy infused her bones.

Irritated by the path of her thoughts, Tess turned her back on the river. Through the open doorway she could see Jean sitting happily once again in front of the television, sipping a fresh cup of tea, her incident with the eggs forgotten. Fletch sat beside her, holding her hand, his dark wavy hair a stark contrast to the thin, white wisps of his mother's.

He looked up at her at that moment and for a second they just stared at each other. Tess felt the melancholy sink into her marrow. Then Fletch raised an eyebrow and she nodded at him and he once again mouthed, 'Thank you,' before kissing his mother gently on the head and easing away from her.

Tess moved inside, following Fletch into the kitchen.

'All sorted?'

She nodded. 'Yes.'

They were standing a couple of metres apart and Fletch took a step towards her as a well of gratitude rising inside him propelled him forward. In the old days he would have swept her into his arms. 'I know this is a big ask, Tess…'

Tess shook her head. If he truly knew, he wouldn't have asked. 'You have no idea, Fletch.'

Just looking at his face caused her chest to ache. It took her back to times she'd spent ten years trying to forget. Ryan had looked so like his father it had been ridiculous. He took another step towards her but she held up her hand to ward him off.

Fletch stopped. 'You think this is any easier for me?' he asked.

Tess dropped her gaze at the honesty in his. It was a horrible situation for them both. 'What time do you want me here in the mornings?'

Tess had no idea where she was going to stay for the next couple of months but she'd figure it out. In the interim she could extend her stay at the hotel. But there was no way her budget could stretch to such luxury for more than a week.

Fletch frowned. 'I don't just want you here in the mornings, Tess, I want you here twenty-four seven.'

Tess's gaze flew back to his face. 'What?' Her heartbeat kicked up a notch as his meaning sank in.

'Mum's wandering more during the night and can become quite agitated when you try and get her back to bed. She's particularly disorientated when she wakes up in the morning since moving from Trish's. She sees me and the first person she asks for in the morning or if she wakes at night is you. It'll be good for her to have you right there when she's so distressed.'

Tess held his gaze. 'And when I go?'

Fletch had always believed in not borrowing trouble. He had it covered for the next two months and that was all he was worried about for now. 'We'll cross that bridge when we get to it,' he said, his expression grim.

'Your mother's condition needs a little more forward planning than that,' she said waspishly.

Dealing with families of dementia sufferers, Tess knew that those who had planned for every contingency coped better with the curve balls the condition threw them.

Fletch nodded. He couldn't agree more. 'Another reason why I need you here. Forward planning.' He looked into her shuttered gaze. 'It makes sense for you to stay here, Tess. And where are you going to find short-term accommodation at such late notice?'

Anywhere but here. 'I have friends in Brisbane…'

'Do you? Do you really, Tess? Kept in contact with the old crowd, have you?'

Tess broke eye contact. He knew she'd severed all links when she'd moved overseas. Before that even, when concerned friends had been too much for her to handle. She'd withdrawn from all her support groups, from her life really, as grief had consumed her utterly.

'I can't pretend happy families with you, Fletch,' she said, the marble surface of the kitchen bench cold beneath her hand. 'Too much has happened. Living with you again…it'll bring too much back.'

Fletch nodded. He knew that. And after only a couple of hours in her company he knew it would be harder than he'd originally thought. But sometimes the greatest gain came at the greatest cost. Ten years ago she'd shut down, shut him out—shut the world out—and he'd let her. With her here and committed to the task she wasn't running away any more and maybe, just maybe, they could face head-on what they hadn't been able to a decade ago.

'You think it's going to matter where you lay your hat each night,' he asked her downcast head, 'when we'll be seeing each other day in and day out?'

Tess knew he was right. It was going to be difficult whether she stayed here or not.

Fletch willed her to look at him. 'We have to prepare ourselves for the fact that this isn't going to be easy, Tess. It *will* bring back painful memories. But if we keep our focus on Mum then I'm sure we'll get through it.' He shrugged. 'Who knows, we might even become friends.' He gave a half-smile. 'I hear that's possible.'

Tess speared him with a look. 'We're not an ordinary divorced couple, Fletch.'

He nodded, acknowledging the truth of her words. 'Still…I never wanted it to be like this between us, Tess.'

Fletch tamped down on the guilt that he kept in a box labelled 'Tess', knowing that ultimately it was he who had severed their relationship. He wished he could go back and undo what he'd done that night nine years ago. That his actions hadn't made their already shaky marriage untenable and guilt hadn't driven him to grab hold of the out she'd given him.

Yes, their relationship breakdown had been multi-factorial and, yes, she had been the one to ask for a divorce, but when it had come to the crunch, he hadn't fought for it.

Or her.

He'd run away—just like she had.

Tess still remembered her surprise at his easy capitulation when she'd asked him for a divorce. 'We don't always get what we want,' she said testily.

He held up his hands in surrender. He didn't want to get into this now. He really didn't.

'This apartment is big enough for all of us, Tess. It would really help Mum and me if you stayed here for the duration.'

Tess would have liked nothing more than to walk away and never see Fletch again. But there was no way she could turn her back on Jean now, and Fletch was right—it was easy and convenient for her to stay here.

She hadn't fought with him nine years ago as they'd calmly ended their marriage—why waste her breath doing so now? She'd do what she had to do then leave—just like she'd done before.

'Fine,' she muttered. 'I'll go and get my stuff.'

An hour later Tess was back from checking out of her hotel and following Fletch as he showed her to her room.

Which looked suspiciously like his room.

'This is your room,' she said bluntly, looking at the signs of his habitation strewn everywhere.

His watch and one of those crime novels he loved to read lay on the bedside table. A desk by the large floor-to-ceiling windows housed a sleek laptop and a tottering pile of papers and medical journals. A tie was thrown over the back of the chair. A pair of socks lay discarded on the thick, expensive-looking carpet.

'Yes. It is.'

Tess stared at him incredulously. 'I am *not* sharing a room with you.'

Fletch clutched his heart in mock injury. 'You wound me.'

'Don't you have another room in this luxury riverside apartment?' She ignored him, crossing her arms. 'And don't you dare lecture me about being adult, about me not having anything you haven't seen before or about keeping the pretence going into the bedroom because this is not negotiable!'

Fletch smiled as her eyes hissed fire at him like a lava flow of molasses. She looked so much like the old Tess for a moment that his breath caught.

Even if he hadn't seen any of what she had in a very, very long time.

'The only other bedroom I have, my mother lives in.'

'This is a two-bedroom apartment? Only two bed-rooms?'

Tess hoped that the squeak she could hear in her voice was just being distorted through the layers of confusion in her brain.

'It's okay, Tess. I'll sleep on the couch. It's perfectly comfortable. Probably better with Mum tending to wander during the night anyway.'

Tess felt a wave of relief wash over her as she sagged against the doorjamb. In fact, she felt a little silly at her reaction that could be seen as being slightly over the top. But, honestly, sharing the apartment with Fletch was bad enough—she didn't even want to contemplate sharing a bed with him too.

She already knew how good that was.

And guilt had driven all the good out of her a lot of years ago.

'I think you're going to need to get yourself some clothes,' Fletch said as he plucked her overnight bag from her fingers and strode across his room, dumping it on his bed.

She nodded. 'I hadn't exactly planned on staying. I'll slip down to a department store in the next couple of days and pick up a few outfits.'

His eyes met hers as he tried not to think about the time she'd dragged him into the change room at a department store on a slow Sunday morning and had had her way with him in front of three mirrors.

He failed.

And if the sudden smoulder in her eyes was anything to go by, so had she.

'I'll let you get settled in,' he said, withdrawing quickly—because he knew from bitter experience that down that path lay no good.

Tess was in bed by eight-thirty. The jet-lag, the wine and the tumult of emotions from the day had well and truly caught up with her. She'd tried really hard to stay awake with Jean and Fletch but in vain. Fletch had nudged her awake and ordered her to bed. She hadn't even bothered to shower or change—just kicked out of her cargo pants and collapsed onto the bed in her knickers and T-shirt, barely getting the covers over her before she sank into the blissful depths of dreamless slumber.

She wasn't sure how many hours had passed when she first heard the commotion. It took Tess a while to realise Jean's sobbing wasn't coming from inside her head as it usually did but externally, outside the room somewhere.

And it was actually real this time.

She sat bolt upright as the shackles of heavy slumber fell from her eyes. The clock said two a.m. as she kicked the covers aside and stumbled out of the room, her heart pounding like a gong.

'Jean?' she called as she hurried down the hallway to her mother-in-law's room.

Nothing. *The bed was empty.*

'Jean?' she said again, louder this time as she headed towards the source of human anguish getting louder and louder.

52   HOW TO MEND A BROKEN HEART

'Out here, Tess,' Fletch called.

Tess entered the lounge area. The lamp near the television threw weak light into the room and she headed to the lounge where Fletch sat comforting his weeping mother.

'Everything okay?'

Fletch nodded over his mother's head as Jean sobbed.

'It's no good, Fletcher,' Jean sobbed. 'No good.'

Tess, her lack of clothing eliminated from her subconscious by nagging fatigue and her pounding heart, crouched down in front of them. 'Hey, Jean, don't cry, sweetie. It's okay.' She rubbed her palms against a pair of bony knees. 'What's the matter?'

Jean turned wet cheeks on Tess. 'You should never let the sun go down on an argument. Never spend a night apart. Fletch's dad and I never spent a night apart.' She grabbed Tess's hand. 'You never know how long you have with each other.'

Tess murmured, 'Of course not,' not entirely sure what was going on.

'I was just telling Mum that I got in late from the hospital and didn't want to disturb you so I collapsed on the couch.'

Ah. Now Tess got the reason for Jean's distress. And it was *acute* distress. She was crying, her movements agitated.

'It's still wrong,' Jean sobbed. 'You don't care about being disturbed, do you, Tess, darling?'

Tess looked at Fletch. He was at his disturbing best. Shirtless and trouserless, his big, bare chest and long, bare, dark-haired legs exuding a masculinity that was almost overwhelming in the intimacy of the little circle they'd formed. He rubbed the back of his neck in a helpless gesture and the lines of worry and tiredness around his eyes and mouth seemed to deepen.

She wished like hell they cancelled out the scruffy sexiness of his tousled hair and unshaven jaw.

'This is how people get divorced,' Jean continued, worrying at the fabric of her nightgown, rolling it between her fingers. She suddenly clutched Tess's arm. 'Oh, no...you're not getting divorced, are you?'

Tess felt her heart sink. Jean's level of anxiety was distressing to watch. As fanciful as it might seem to them, she was worrying herself sick.

And for that there was just one thing she could do.

She took a deep breath and slid her hand onto Fletch's knee and then up a little further to his thigh. 'Of course not, Jean,' Tess murmured, not acknowledging either his harshly indrawn breath or the tensing of his firm, bulky quadriceps. 'Fletch and I are fine, aren't we, darling?'

She looked at him then and smiled, sincerely hoping he could act better than she could.

CHAPTER FOUR

FLETCH was too stunned to say anything for a moment. His body, on the other hand, wasn't as reticent. Her hand searing into his flesh took him back to the days when they hadn't been able to stop touching each other and in an instant he was hard.

A decade ago she'd have sensed his arousal in a flash with that weird sexual ESP they'd shared. She would have smiled at him, moved her hand slowly up his leg and kept going until she'd hit pay dirt.

'Fletch?'

He blinked as Tess's voice yanked him back to the here and now. To the startling reality of the present—Tess hadn't wanted him in a very long time and his mother was sitting right beside him.

His very distressed mother.

Grateful he was sitting down, Fletch grappled with what exactly the question had been.

'We're fine, aren't we?' Tess prompted, squeezing the firm, warm muscle beneath her palm.

Fletch saw the *keep up* look in her amber gaze as he fought against the automatic impulse to shut his eyes. Her little squeeze had shot straight to his groin like a blast from a taser. God, he was too tired for this. He'd tossed and turned on the couch for hours.

'Of course we are,' he agreed heartily as he picked up the thread of the conversation. He covered Tess's hand with his own. 'I really just didn't want to disturb you, that's all.'

Jean's fretting eased as she patted their joined hands. 'You're such a sweet boy, darling, but, trust me, sleeping on the couch can be the beginning of a slippery slope. Look at Aunty Lynne, she and Joe sleep in different bedrooms now because of his snoring and they can barely stand the sight of each other. That all started at the couch, you know.'

Fletch glanced at Tess, his sexual frustration tempered by his feelings of helplessness. Did he tell his mother that both Lynne, his father's sister, and her husband Joe had died in the last few years?

Tess saw the inadequacy in his gaze and squeezed his thigh again. This could not be easy for him. 'Well, Fletch doesn't snore,' she said, diverting the conversation, 'so I think we'll be fine.' She gave Jean a wry smile. 'Now, how about a mug of nice warm milk?'

'Good idea,' Fletch said, leaping at the opportunity to escape the steady torture of her hand.

He reached for his trousers, desperate for some more cover. Tess's foot anchored one leg to the floor and she stood to release it. But then her bare thighs were at eye level. And even though they were thinner than he remembered—ballerina thin—and skinny wasn't something that had ever really appealed to him, his hard-on didn't seem to care, especially given how a quick flick of his eyes upwards also put her knickers squarely in his line of vision.

He looked down and hurriedly stuffed his feet into the legs of his trousers. He rose quickly, not looking at her, dragging them up his legs and over his hips in one fluid moment, zipping the fly as he took his first stride away.

'I'll make them. Sit down,' he threw over his shoulder as he headed towards the kitchen. And sanity.

Tess felt a blush creep up her cheeks and was grateful for the low light as she sank down next to Jean. She wished she hadn't caught his heated gaze on her thighs or that brief glimpse of the bulge being contained by his underwear—but she had.

He was aroused?

Mugs clattered in the background and Jean chatted away beside her, oblivious to Tess's internal conflict as she grappled with the incident. Had her touch, her completely artificial touch, on his leg done that?

It had been too long surely? Too much had happened between them. Too much angst. Too much sorrow.

Yes, Fletch had always been a very virile man and their sex life had always been firmly in the mind-blowing category. Nothing had seemed to dent it. Not shift work, pregnancy or living with a newborn.

Until Ryan's death anyway.

And then it had all changed. She just…couldn't. She'd barely been able to eat or string a sentence together for so long. Anything beyond that, anything requiring any kind of emotional energy or physical effort, had been too much.

And Fletcher had been understanding and patient.

But in the end it had defeated him.

Or at least she'd thought so. Until now. Seeing the evidence of his arousal had been startling. Was that just a normal male reaction to the proximity of a semi-clad woman or could he still really desire her after all these years?

It was a shocking concept.

A dangerous one.

The microwave dinged behind her and Tess dragged her thoughts away from her ex-husband's libido. It certainly wasn't something she was going to analyse. Now or at any other time.

'Okay, three warm milks coming up,' Fletch announced, placing the beverages on the coffee table.

Tess pushed everything aside as she picked up her mug and pulled her recalcitrant thoughts firmly back to Jean.

After leaving his mother with assurances that he would be returning to the marital bed, Fletch did indeed head to his room. Tess had volunteered to settle Jean back to sleep and he needed a shower.

He hadn't had one earlier as he hadn't wanted to disturb her. Sure, he could have had one in the main bathroom but all his stuff, his toiletries and clothes, were in his bedroom so he'd put it off till morning. But after the events of the night, after his involuntary reaction to her, he was prescribing himself a cold shower.

A quick, cold shower.

In and out before Tess even knew he was there. His mother often took quite some time to settle once she'd been wandering—the darkness exacerbating her dementia—so he should be well and truly clear before Tess came back.

Not that he wanted to be thinking about his ex-wife as he shed his clothes and stepped into the shower. Or what had happened at her tentative touch. Things started to stir again and he turned the cold spray on full bore, sucking in a breath as the icy spray pelted his flesh.

He dunked his head beneath the shower head, squeezing his eyes shut. He absolutely didn't need this.

Whatever the hell this was.

Some latent attraction? A vestige of what they'd once shared? Those endless hours in each other's arms, making love like the world was about to end, like their skin was brushed with crack cocaine and they *just couldn't get enough.*

Fletch shook his head against images that usually only visited him in his dreams. It was dangerous ground.

He turned so the spray drummed hard down his back, hoping it would scour the memories from his pores. Praying they'd sluice off his skin and disappear for ever down the drain hole.

But the drumming in his head mocked even louder.

Tess. Tess. Tess.

Tess sat with Jean for a while after she'd fallen asleep, surprised that her ex-mother-in-law had gone down as easily as she had. Surprised but relieved. Many a night she'd spent with an Alzheimer's patient trying to calm them so they'd sleep and it was rarely an easy task.

Tess was so tired when she entered the bedroom she almost missed the sound of the shower. She blinked as she stared at the closed en suite door.

Fletch?

She didn't move for a moment as a sense of déjà vu swept through her. Walking into their bedroom, the shower running.

Of course, once upon a time she'd have pushed open the door—not that Fletch would have bothered with shutting it—stripped off her clothes and joined him.

Which wasn't an option now.

But what the hell was? This *was* his room.

She was the intruder.

She clutched at her abdomen to allay the funny tightness building there. Her fingers hit warm flesh and she looked down absently at her clothes, or lack of them. She remembered how her bare thighs had burned beneath his gaze earlier. How his body had responded...

Her legs sparked into action. She could at least get into her pyjamas. She opened her carry-on case, which was all she'd thought she'd need for her whistle-stop foray back to Australia, and located the over-sized man's T-shirt she wore to bed. She'd got into the habit of wearing Fletch's T-shirts to bed during their marriage and, out of comfort, had continued the practice.

Not that they belonged to him any longer. Or any other man, for that matter. Her men's shirts these days came to her courtesy of the men's department at a store.

With the shower still obviously running, she whisked off the T-shirt she had on and threw the other one over her head. It came to mid-thigh and she felt infinitely more covered even if it was too broad across the chest, causing it to constantly fall off her shoulder and the V-neck to hang too low on her bra-enhanced cleavage.

She scrambled into the bed—Fletcher's bed—getting under the covers this time, and waited for him, her eyes firmly trained on the en suite door. It didn't matter how tired she was, that her eyes felt like they'd been rolled in shell grit, that the room seemed to tilt precariously every now and then.

Or that something had happened before that had the potential to be a real problem between them.

They needed to talk. About Jean.

Sitting with her before, Tess had come to a decision. A crazy one for sure, but the right one nonetheless. She and Fletch needed to have a conversation—no matter how difficult the subject matter. And the sooner they had it, the sooner she could get to sleep.

All providing she actually could sleep if he agreed to what she had to say.

The door opened suddenly and she took a deep, steadying breath.

Fletch's breath hissed out as he spied Tess sitting up in his bed, looking exhausted but grimly determined and somehow sexy as hell with her huge amber eyes and one shoulder bare except for a narrow bra strap.

'Oh, God, sorry, I thought you'd still be in with Mum...'

Tess didn't drop her gaze to take in her fill of his bare chest or the long length of his legs not covered by the boxer shorts. But she was uncomfortably aware of them in her peripheral vision.

'It's okay,' she said softly. 'Jean went straight off to sleep. She was exhausted.'

The tension coiling the muscles in Fletch's neck as tight as piano wire eased a little. Already the decision to ask Tess to stay seemed to have paid off. 'Thank you. You're great with her.'

His mother had never settled so quickly for him.

Unfortunately it wasn't enough to fully dissipate the tightness in his neck. And after his reaction to her earlier, he doubted it ever would. Not while they were living under the same roof.

Still, keeping focused on the reason why she was there—his mother—and keeping as much distance as was possible inside the confines of his apartment, Fletch figured he could just about survive it.

Tess pulled the shirt sleeve up onto her shoulder. *That helped.*

It promptly slid off again. *Oh, boy...*

'So…' He hesitated. He didn't know why. 'Goodnight, then…see you in the morning.'

He turned to go but her soft 'Fletcher' pulled him up short. He turned back and quirked an eyebrow. 'Yes?'

'I think you should sleep in here with me.'

Fletch could have sworn he actually heard the synapses in his brain misfire. Certainly for quite a few moments he was struck completely dumb.

Well, this sure blew the distance ploy out of the water.

Tess watched as a range of emotions flitted across her ex-husband's face. Did he think she'd suggest something so out there if she didn't think it was absolutely necessary?

'We can't have a repeat of tonight, Fletch.'

Fletch shrugged. There'd been so many disrupted nights like this since he and his mother had moved into the apartment two weeks before, it seemed normal to him now. Still, the sentiment weighed heavily in his mind.

'She's not going to remember what happened in the morning.'

Tess raised her legs beneath the covers, tenting them as she propped her chin on her knees. 'I know. But do you want her to go through the same distressing anxiety every time she wanders in the middle of the night and finds you on the couch?'

Fletch knew the short answer was no. Of course he didn't. And Tess's solution was, obviously, a quick, simple fix. But nothing had been simple between them for a long time.

They were bereaved, aggrieved and divorced.

That was a whole lot of baggage to take with them to a bed they hadn't shared in nine years.

'If you're not on the couch,' she continued, 'there's no reason for any distress.'

Tess projected a calm, measured professionalism, like she was talking to a relative of a patient, but on the inside the mere thought of what she was suggesting was making her quake. She hadn't seen him in nine years and now she was proposing they share the same bed. Maybe she'd wake up in the morning and it would have all been a bad dream.

She was used to that.

Fletch hastily diverted his gaze from the bed, mentally sizing up the room. 'I suppose I could sleep on the floor...'

Tess could barely hear him over the thudding of her heart, like a drum in her ears. She knew he was trying to do the right thing but did he really have to look at the bed like it was a viper's nest?

Did he really think *she* wanted to share the thing with *him*?

'Don't be ridiculous, Fletch,' she dismissed impatiently. 'You can't sleep on the floor for two months.'

Fletch lifted his gaze to meet hers. 'So...to be clear. You're suggesting that I sleep in the bed. With you?'

Not a suggestion he'd ever imagined he'd hear coming from her mouth ever again. The tension in his shoulders headed south to grab a stranglehold on his gut.

Tess heard the note of incredulity in his voice and shrugged. 'Will it really be *that* difficult to sleep with me again?'

Fletch swallowed hard, the knowledge of his recent monster erection colouring his reasoning. 'No.' He gave a self-deprecating smile. 'That's what I'm worried about.'

Tess couldn't help but be amused at the absurdity of

it all and the rather sceptical look on Fletch's face. He'd always been so decisive, so take-charge, it was a novelty to see him so completely flummoxed.

Her mouth kicked up at one side briefly before returning to a determined line. 'We're not teenagers, Fletch. I'm not proposing reconciliation. We're just two adults making the best out of a less-than-satisfactory situation. I'm sure we can control ourselves.'

Fletch heroically refrained from mentioning that controlling herself when they were in bed together had never been a forte of hers.

Or of his.

Not until after Ryan's death anyway. Her control then had been savage. She'd stopped needing him, stopped wanting him, overnight.

But he'd still needed her. So very, very much. More than that—he'd needed her to need him back.

Fletch stood at the end of the bed, still hesitating as a decade of distance yawned between them. 'I could put a roll or something down the middle of the bed,' he suggested.

Tess surprised herself with her laugh. 'How very Victorian.'

He laughed back. 'I thought a fan of Georgette Heyer would appreciate it.'

Their smiles lit the room briefly then slowly faded. Tess sighed. 'It's almost three in the morning and I'm jet-lagged to hell and back, Fletch. I'm too tired for this conversation. Just get into bed.'

He nodded, coming to a decision. She was right. It *was* half past stupid hour. And they *were* adults. 'Okay. Let me just check everything's locked up one more time.'

Fletch went through his usual pre-bed door-checking

routine. It was a particular nightmare of his that his mother would manage to find her way onto the balcony during one of her many night-time walkies and plunge to her death.

Still he lingered over it, his heart pounding loud enough to wake the whole building. Certainly loud enough to wake his mother.

He was about to sleep with his ex-wife. With Tess. And even though it wasn't sexual, he felt like a virgin again, like he was sleeping with a woman for the first time.

Satisfied everything was locked up tight and unable to put it off any longer, Fletch made his way to his bedroom, quickly checking on his mother as he turned appropriately neutral opening sentences over and over in his head.

Something to break the ice.

Decrease the awkwardness that she surely must feel as keenly as him. Something like *What's the weather like in Devonshire at the moment?* Or *How about those English cricketers?*

Fletch stopped in the hallway just shy of his door and allowed an internal groan free rein.

How lame!

But anything was better than *Take all your clothes off and let me make love to you.*

Because a few lousy hours back in her company and the imperative to be with her, to peel off her clothes and bury himself inside her, was raging in his blood like a fever. It was a bad time to discover she was a habit that he'd never managed to shake.

It had been ten years and he wanted her as much now as he ever had.

Guilt, hot and fierce, rose in him and he squeezed

his eyes shut to dispel the images of their intertwined
bodies.

He didn't deserve her.

He had proved himself unworthy.

He took a deep, steadying breath, shaking off the tug
of dark memories and guilt, and stepped into the bedroom. But whatever pithy comment had been on the tip
of his tongue died before even a syllable was spoken
and he sagged against the jamb as a knot of tension released like the strings of a marionette.

Tess was asleep.

Sound asleep if her soft snore was any indication.

She lay on her side, knees tucked up, sheet anchored
beneath her arms. The bedside lamps threw shadows
that darkened the hollows of her cheeks and the smudges
beneath her eyes. Even in slumber she looked like she
carried the weight of the world on her shoulders.

He watched her for a long time, keeping his distance. Knowing he'd do anything to erase her burden.
Wishing that he could go back to this day ten years ago
and fix the damn lock, take away her migraine, remove
the bucket, stop the overnight deluge, make the ambulance come faster.

Feeling again the rage and the helplessness. His
complete impotency that when it had counted most, he
hadn't been able to protect his family.

He squeezed his eyes shut, pushing his thumb and
forefingers hard into the lids, blocking the images. God,
he was tired. So very tired.

He needed perspective.

He needed sleep.

He pushed away from the jamb and drew level with
the bed. Slowly he eased himself onto it, being careful

not to disturb her, sticking close to the edge and lying as stiff as a centuries-old mummy.

After a moment he slowly turned his head to look at her. Or her back anyway. Once upon a time he would have reached out and stroked his hand down the notches of her spine, drawn her in closer. Instead he turned away and reached for the lamp switch, extinguishing both with one action, plunging the room into darkness.

She stirred and he held his breath. She muttered in her sleep, rolled over, settled again. She was closer now. And facing him. He could feel her breath fanning his shoulder and as his eyes adjusted to the darkness he could make out the outline of her mouth.

Great.

Fletch rolled his head back until he was staring at the ceiling. There weren't that many more hours left in the night. But he had a feeling he was going to see every one of them.

He did finally fall into an exhausted sleep just as dawn was spreading its first blush across a fading night sky. After lying tense and unmoving for a couple of hours, listening to her breathe, his body finally succumbed to its baser dictates and slowly relaxed into the folds of slumber.

Unfortunately, thanks to those baser dictates, it didn't last long. They didn't seem to mind that he'd had less than four hours' sleep all night. All they cared about was that it was morning, something warm, soft and female was snuggled into him, his hand was full of a smooth, clad buttock and a certain part of his anatomy was wide awake.

Fletch's eyes flew open as every muscle contracted

in painful unison. His heart pounded in his chest as, for a brief moment, total disorientation reigned.

Then Tess moved a little, readjusting her head against the ball of his shoulder, murmuring something nonsensical, her lips grazing his skin, her hand skating close, too close, to his painfully tight erection.

And he was suddenly one hundred per cent orientated.

His first instinct was to leap out of the bed like the mattress had caught fire. He doubted Tess would appreciate that they didn't have control of their bodily functions while under the influence of sleep and he had no desire to have her accuse him of taking advantage of the situation.

He'd realised yesterday just how hard this was going to be, but with her draped all over him, this was a whole other level of difficult. Too many mornings like this and he might just forget the reason she was there. Forget that this was fake and they were only pretending for his mother's sake.

He had to be careful they didn't cross a line—even in their sleep—because emotionally he didn't think she was up to it.

And he knew for sure he wasn't.

But right at this moment she was hard to resist. Her head was tucked into his shoulder, her breath was warm on his bare pec and she was all soft and supple against him. And his nostrils were full of her—passionfruit, honey and something else distinctly feminine.

He drew in a deep steady breath, sucking her deep into his lungs, savouring her.

Tess had always smelled so good.

So he didn't move. Not yet. He would—soon.

But not yet.

* * *

Tess woke slowly through myriad layers of a heavy sleep surrounded by a feeling of heat and solidness, a powerful malaise infecting her bones. She chased the last vestiges of a dream she couldn't quite remember across the fading edges of her sleep like a child would chase the tail of an escaped balloon as it rose in the sky.

She murmured a protest—her dreams were so rarely good and she fought against the sticky fingers that were trying to drag her away from the tail, back into the world of the conscious.

A hand curving around her bottom was comforting and she wriggled into it, bending her knee higher, revelling in the hairy bulk of a leg under it. Her lips brushed against firm, warm skin and an earthy aroma, very male, tickled her nostrils.

Hmm. Fletch had always smelled so good.

Beneath her hand, a solid slab of flat muscle undulated and tensed as if it was agitated. She smoothed it absently, stroking it lightly. Her fingers brushed something hard, something familiar and it twitched against her hand.

She frowned. *Something very familiar.*

The last strand of sleep fell with a loud clang like a metal shackle.

Fletch?

Her hand froze. The breath hitched in her lungs. Her eyes opened with a start. She was instantly awake, instantly aware of her situation.

She pushed away from Fletch abruptly, scrambling back to her side of the bed like an epileptic crab until her back hit the bedhead and she yanked the sheet up to her chin.

'What the hell?' she demanded, glaring at him.

Fletch glared back as he too boosted himself up

against the bedhead. Okay, he was guilty of not separating from her earlier but no way was she going to make him the big bad wolf when she was the one draped against him with her fingerprints all over his belly.

'It's the morning,' he said defensively. 'It happens.'

Particularly if a woman is rubbing herself against me like a great big tabby cat.

Tess fought the urge to blush as she remembered how many times his biological wake-up call had led to a little morning glory. He looked so virile with his tousled hair, his big bare chest and his frown but, still, she couldn't believe she'd been...pawing at him. She dropped her gaze.

Fletch wasn't satisfied. 'You were the one touching me,' he reminded her downcast head for good measure.

Tess nodded, mortified at her behaviour. He was right.

They were divorced, for crying out loud!

'Yes.' She looked up at him. 'I'm so sorry, I was... dreaming and... God! Sorry.'

Fletch sighed at her obvious embarrassment. He should have known this was going to happen, that their bodies would naturally gravitate towards each other. That they'd subconsciously seek affection.

He rubbed a hand through his hair. 'No...I'm sorry. It's just... I don't know, Tess. It was probably inevitable. Our bodies were just reverting to type, I guess... in sleep...'

She knew what he was saying was most likely correct but it had still been a shock. She'd known last night when she'd felt the heat of his gaze on her thighs that they were on shaky ground. The fact that he didn't look any happier about it than she helped.

She grimaced. 'Maybe we're going to need that roll between us in the bed after all.'

Fletch was momentarily taken aback by her glum observation. Then he chuckled, tension slowly oozing from his muscles. 'Maybe we just need to realise that we can't control what we do when we're asleep and not get ourselves in a tizz about it when we wake up.'

Tess look affronted, crossing her arms. 'I did not get in a tizz.'

Fletch chuckled again as he threw back the sheet and swung his legs to the floor. 'Oh, you were in a tizz all right.'

'You don't have to leave, Fletch,' she said as he stood and the mattress shifted a little beneath her. It was *his* bed, for crying out loud. 'I promise no more tizzies in future.'

He looked down at her. 'Are you sure? Because if there's one thing I've learned over the years it's that morning hard-ons are part and parcel of being a man. Are you okay with that or should I buy myself a sleeping bag?'

Tess swallowed. She hadn't had a single sexual urge in a decade. She doubted her libido, weird dreams aside, would be a problem. But he was giving her a choice. Which would be a lot easier to make if it hadn't felt so good being pressed against him just now.

She thought she'd suppressed those feelings a long time ago.

Obviously not.

Still, she couldn't let him sleep on the floor in a sleeping bag when there was enough room for both of them in the bed. She swallowed. 'I'm okay with it.' They just needed to be careful, that's all. 'As long as you keep them on your side of the bed.'

Fletch nodded. *Fair enough.* 'I'll check on Mum.'

Tess watched him go. Watched the strong lines of his bare back as he disappeared out the door. She shook her head to clear it. To try and grasp the rapid events that had led to her being back in her ex's bed.

Yesterday morning her life had been on track. It hadn't been rock-'n'-roll exciting but she liked it that way. Today she'd been sucked back into her baggage-laden past. Not a place she would ever have volunteered to visit.

But she'd told Fletch she'd do it for Jean and she'd meant it. And if that meant she had to be on her guard, even in her sleep, well, she guessed she could hack it for two months.

Determined to divert her thoughts, she sank down into the bed, thinking about her mother-in-law, already planning a schedule and thinking of ways things could be made a little easier.

'Still out to it,' Fletch announced as he re-entered the room a minute or so later. 'She usually sleeps late the morning after a disturbed night.'

Tess nodded. 'I've just been thinking about that,' she mused, surprised to feel the urge to check out his naked chest. 'I may have something that could help.'

'Oh?'

'What does the lease say about pets?'

CHAPTER FIVE

AFTER the embarrassment of their early-morning start, the day flew by. Tess took advantage of Fletch's flexible working hours and went out as soon as the shops opened. Nothing to do with needing some breathing space—*not at all*—and everything to do with needing some clothes.

She spent a couple of hours bargain hunting to extend her meagre wardrobe and did a bit of a grocery shop. Jean had always liked to cook and there was no reason why she still couldn't do so with Tess around to 'help'.

So she brought some basics that were needed for the meal plan she and Fletch had worked out whilst trying to make awkward conversation over breakfast and extras for daily baking, which had always been a particular favourite of Jean's. In fact, Jean had been a champion cake-icer in her day so Tess made sure she included those ingredients in the trolley. Hopefully this skill could be nurtured and retained for as long as possible.

So much about Alzheimer's was focused on what the sufferer couldn't do, couldn't remember, instead of making the most of what they could.

She did not think about Fletch and their early-morning predicament. Or at least every time she did she stopped herself. Denial she was good at.

Denial she'd perfected.

And having to pretend they were happily married was something well worth denying.

When Tess got home Fletch went into St Rita's for a few hours to meet with the ethics committee over the parameters of his study. It wasn't his favourite part of the research process but a very necessary evil that not only protected trial subjects but also himself and the hospital from any potential liability.

When he was done he accompanied Tess and his mother to get the pet Tess assured him would help with Jean's anxiety. He was still sceptical as they entered the animal shelter and were greeted by a cacophony of barking but when Jean's face lit up he had to concede it might have merit.

Jean looked at them. 'What are we doing here?'

'We're getting a kitten,' Fletch said patiently for the tenth time in the last thirty minutes.

Jean beamed at him. 'Really?' She clapped her hands together. 'Can I go and look?'

Tess laughed at Jean's childlike relish, feeling vindicated. It had been a hard sell talking Fletch into flagrantly disregarding the lease agreement but she'd seen with her own eyes how much difference a pet could make in the life of someone suffering from dementia and had refused to be easily deterred.

When presented with the evidence, of which she could quote both anecdotal and scientific verbatim, Fletch had reluctantly agreed. She would have liked to push for a dog but common sense and apartment living took precedence and she'd suggested a house-trained cat.

'Of course. Go ahead.' Tess grinned. 'We'll just have a quick chat to the attendant and be along in a moment.'

When Tess and Fletch spotted Jean ten minutes later she was crouched down in front of a cage, talking animatedly to the animal inside. 'Oh, look, darling.' Jean waved at her son impatiently to move faster. 'It's Tabby.'

Tess quickened her steps, smiling at Jean's eagerness. It seemed Jean had already chosen her kitten and named it!

'Thank goodness you found her,' Jean told the shelter attendant following closely behind Tess. 'I didn't realise she'd gone missing. Trish would be worried sick if she knew her beloved Tabby dog had wandered away.'

Tess frowned. *Dog?* They drew level with the cage and looked down at a chunky, white-whiskered, ancient golden Labrador.

'You obviously haven't starved while you've been away, have you, girl?' Jean tutted. She poked her bony fingers through the cage wire to stroke the dog's ear. The dog whined appreciatively and angled its head for Jean to reach the sweet spot.

'Tabby?' Tess murmured to Fletch.

'Childhood dog of Trish's. She thought she was getting a cat and already had the name picked out,' he said quietly.

Tess pressed her lips together to suppress a smile, not game to say a word.

'Yes,' he said testily. 'The irony is not lost on me.'

'Come on, then, girl.' Jean gave the yellow-grey head one last scratch and stood. 'Let's get you home.'

Fletch looked askance at the dog. Putting aside that he lived in a nineteenth-floor apartment, the Lab looked like it was going to expire any moment either from old age or a triglyceride-induced heart attack. Maybe both.

He shook his head and muttered, 'Great,' as he sent Tess a *fix this* glare.

A bubble of laughter surged into her chest and Tess bit the side of her cheek to prevent its escape. It felt good to have the spectre of their living arrangements temporarily removed from the forefront of her brain by something so frivolous. 'Er, Jean,' Tess said, gently cupping Jean's elbow and leading her towards the next cage. 'We're here for a kitten, remember? Let's have a look around a bit more first, hey?'

And hopefully forget all about the dog.

Jean dug her feet in and looked at her reproachfully. 'Tessa! We can't leave Tabby here. Trish would be heart-broken. She belongs at home.'

Tess flicked a glance at the dog, which looked at her steadily with those big brown eyes, then at Fletch. He shook his head very firmly from side to side. 'We agreed on a cat,' he murmured in a low voice. Like a rumble of thunder.

Tess rolled her eyes. 'Okay, sure,' she soothed, turning back to Jean. 'We can take her home but how about looking at some cats as well? Look,' she said, pointing to a nearby cage containing a very playful kitten pouncing on a squeaky toy. 'Isn't that little fella cute?'

Jean turned to her son. 'Fletcher,' she admonished, wringing her hands, her voice high and worried. 'It's Tabby. We can't just leave her here!' She sank to the ground in front of the obese, elderly Labrador's cage and rocked slightly on her haunches. 'It's okay, Tabby, I'll get you out of here.'

Tess shrugged at him as Fletch rubbed a hand through his hair. His frustration wafted towards her in almost tangible waves.

'Maybe I can help?' the attendant, a middle-aged woman, intervened. 'I know you had your hearts set on a cat but you came here looking for a companion for your mother who suffers from dementia, right?'

Fletch nodded and she continued.

'Then you really can't go past old Queenie here. She was brought in two days ago after her owner of fourteen years, an elderly lady, died in hospital. Queenie had lain next to her owner, who had taken a fall and broken her hip, all night and into the next day. The lady said that Queenie had refused to leave her side until the community nurse arrived. She'd be a perfect companion for your mother.'

Tess felt goose-bumps prick her skin at the touching story. She watched Jean's agitated movements settle as she stroked Tabby/Queenie's head and murmured to her. What else did they need to make up their minds?

'How did she come to be here?' Tess asked.

'The lady's son brought her in. He travels a lot and doesn't have the time required to care for an arthritic, deaf dog.'

'Deaf?' Fletch shook his head. *Of course.* Queenie was a walking disaster zone.

'Yes.' The attendant smiled. 'She's old and fat. She has arthritic hips and is deaf. She's no pretty young thing, that's for sure. But that just makes her even more ideal for your mum. She's used to being a companion to an elderly lady. She's not young and spritely requiring someone young and spritely to keep up with her. She's content to sit and just be. And she's loyal to a fault.' The woman folded her arms across her chest. 'You won't regret it. Mark my words.'

Tess nodded heartily in agreement, also folding her arms. She turned beseeching eyes on Fletch. He gave her an exasperated look. 'I live on the nineteenth floor.'

'She's fully toilet trained,' the attendant jumped in.

'And exercise is good for Alzheimer sufferers,' Tess added. 'We can go for a few walks a day so Queenie can do her business. It'll be a good routine for Jean as well.'

Fletch looked down at the dog who looked up at him, flopped her head to the side, thumped her tail twice and whined at him, leading him to suspect that she probably wasn't all that deaf.

But three women, four if he counted Queenie, were looking at him like he was lower than a snake's belly, and he knew when he was outgunned.

'Okay, Mum.' He sighed, looking down at her. 'Let's get Qu—Tabby home.' He helped Tess get his mother to her feet and met her sparkling amber gaze above Jean's snowy head. She grinned at him and he growled, 'Smarty pants,' at her.

But as they filled out the paperwork and he watched his mother sitting in the waiting area, stroking a contented-looking Tabby, he couldn't help but smile. Because despite what his lease said, he could already see how the dog had a calming effect on his mother.

And that was most definitely worth it.

It was midnight when Fletch headed to bed. He'd been working on study paperwork—or at least that was what he'd been telling himself. He hadn't exactly been very productive. Tess had been out on her feet early this evening and he'd ordered her to bed at seven.

It had been hard to think about anything else since. Other than her, *Tess*, in his bed.

And how they'd ended up this morning.

And how they might end up tomorrow morning.

But she'd been asleep for a good five hours now. She should be completely immersed in the land of nod. God knew, he was so tired he could barely see straight.

He looked in on his mother as he passed her room
and lingered in the doorway for a moment. She was
curled on her side, her snowy hair visible in the moon-
light streaming through her window. Her hand rested on
Tabby's dozing head. Just then the dog shifted, looked
behind her straight at him and again Fletch wondered
just how deaf their deaf dog really was.

She gave a quiet whine and Fletch said in a low voice,
'It's okay, Tabby, it's just me. Good girl. You come and
let me know if Jean gets out of bed, okay?'

Tabby thumped her tail twice and whined again in
what Fletch could only assume, what he hoped, was
agreement then laid her head back on the bed. He smiled
to himself and continued down the hallway to his bedroom.

Tess was sitting up in bed, reading his detective
novel, when he entered. 'Oh…sorry,' he said. 'I thought
you were asleep.'

She looked up from the book. 'I was, but you know
how jet-lag is. I woke an hour ago like I'd been asleep
for a week and I checked on Jean and I tried to go back
to sleep but I couldn't so…I thought I'd read.'

'Yeah,' he murmured, trying not to look at her bare
shoulder. 'Jet-lag can be a real pain like that.'

Tess nodded. 'It's awful.' Every year it took two
weeks to recover from her three-day jaunt to the other
side of the world.

Fletch stood for a few more moments as the silence
grew between them. 'Anyway, I just came to have a
shower and then get back to it.' He resigned himself to
another night of little sleep—there was no way he could
crawl into bed with her while she was still awake. It was
too…happy families.

And they hadn't been that in a very long time.

She nodded. 'Sure.' And dropped her eyes back to the page she was reading.

Tess was aware of him disappearing into the en suite in her peripheral vision and breathed a sigh of relief when he was gone.

It was going to be a long couple of months.

She steadfastly ignored the sound of the shower as she read the same page three times. It was bound to be awkward for a while. Especially being back in bed together. It wasn't easy pushing the memories away as she always did when he was right there beside her, a very painful reminder.

And not just the memories of Ryan, but of them.

Especially after this morning.

But she'd committed to help with Jean. And it wasn't for ever—it would get easier.

Fletch made sure he had a shirt on as well as his boxers before stepping back into the bedroom. Tess, still reading, looked up from the book. He stayed in the doorframe, leaning his shoulder against the jamb, and smiled at her. 'Since when do you read detective novels?'

Tess shrugged. 'It was that or one of those very scintillating medical journals on your desk.'

Fletch chuckled. 'They may have been more conducive to sleep.'

She smiled. 'Actually, I personally find articles on the latest mitochondrial studies and or DNA sequencing real page-turners.'

Fletch threw his head back and gave a deep belly laugh and for a moment Tess couldn't breathe. How long had it been since she'd heard that sexy laugh?

Ten years? Since just before Ryan had died?

The long tanned column of his throat, sprinkled with

dark whiskers, drew her gaze. Her nipples tightened as an image of her rising from the bed, crossing the room and kissing it took her by surprise.

What the hell?

She blinked rapidly to dispel it.

'Mum seems very settled tonight with Tabby curled up beside her.'

His calm observation dragged her out of a quagmire of confusion. She nodded absently whilst she sorted through appropriate responses.

'I think we're onto a winner there,' she said as her faculties returned. 'Tabby's stuck really close to Jean. It was great to see them sitting on the couch earlier, watching television together, Tabby's head resting on Jean's knee.'

Fletch nodded. 'It was a little confusing for Trish, though, when Mum rang her to tell her we'd found Tabby and she really needed to take better care of her dog.'

They laughed together this time. Listening to the one-sided telephone call had been comical. Tess was just pleased that Trish had caught on fast and knew enough to go along with her mother's false reality.

'Sorry,' she apologised after her laughter had died away. 'It's awful to laugh at something like this.'

Fletch shrugged. What could they do? This thing was happening to them whether they liked it or not. There was a long row to hoe and they needed some relief from the grim reality of it all.

He knew that better than anyone.

'Gotta laugh or you cry, right?' he said philosophically.

Tess didn't respond. What could she say? She'd made a decision when she'd moved to England to lock her grief away and try and get on with things. And it had worked for her. But there wasn't a whole lot of laughter in her life.

'Anyway, I hope it's a sign of things to come,' Fletch continued. 'Mum being this settled.'

Tess shook herself out of her reverie. 'I'm sure it will be. Studies show there is much less nocturnal wandering where pets are present. And even if the person does wander, the theory is that the pet will wake also and either stay with the person or raise the alarm.'

Fletch snorted. 'Except we got ourselves a deaf dog.'

Tess smiled. 'Dogs sense these things intuitively. I think Tabby's already bonded with your mother. I think she already knows, somehow, that Jean needs looking after.'

Fetch didn't answer and Tess wondered if his thoughts had turned to another dog in another time, as hers had.

Memories of Patch, the little Jack Russell terrier that Ryan had been given for his first birthday, arose unbidden. How he'd tried to alert them to what was happening to Ryan that dreadful day.

How he'd tried to save Ryan.

It still hurt to think about her son's faithful companion, about that day, and how she'd blamed Patch for so long for not doing enough. Not barking earlier. Not trying hard enough. But Ryan had adored his puppy dog and suddenly she needed to know what had happened to him.

'Did you take Patch to Canada with you?' she asked into the silence.

Fletch shook his head. 'Trish took him for me. He died from a snake bite a few years ago.'

'Oh.' Tess's guilt at how she'd shunned Patch flared

to life again. But the little dog had just been one more painful reminder she hadn't been able to bear to look at.

Fletch watched a series of emotions chase shadows across her face. 'He did his best, Tess,' he murmured gently. 'The bucket was wedged into the corner of the sandpit and weighted in the bottom with sand. It was heavy and he was a little dog.'

Fletch remembered it as if it was yesterday. Patch's incessant barking, something different about the tone of it waking him even before he'd heard Tess's frantic 'Fletch!'. Tearing out of the house just behind her into the back yard as a blur of brown and white hurled itself at the bucket over and over, toppling it as they reached him, disgorging water and sand and a pale, blue-lipped Ryan.

Tess shut her eyes, shutting down the images of her shaking Ryan, of the rag-doll feel of him against her chest. 'I know.' She nodded. 'I know.'

Fletch wanted to go to her. But, like at the cemetery for the last nine years, he held himself back. She didn't look any more open to his comfort now than she had all those years ago and he'd been rejected too many times to travel down that road again. So he gripped the jamb and waited for her to regain her composure.

She opened her eyes and grimaced at him. 'Sorry.'

Fletch shook his head. 'Don't be. This is hard for both of us but…thank you. Thank you so much for doing this for me. I know it's not easy being here with us again, reminding you of things you don't want to be reminded of.'

He'd hated it that Tess had shut him out in that year after Ryan's death. She'd decided the only way to cope had been avoidance and it hadn't mattered that he'd wanted to talk about it.

Had needed to talk about it.

To talk about Ryan.

She hadn't been able to even bear having his name mentioned so he'd stopped trying and internalised everything and they'd grown further and further apart.

So he knew that being here, being confronted by him every day, had to be challenging for her. He just hadn't realised how challenging it was going to be for him as well.

'It's fine, Fletch.'

Dredging up the past was something she'd avoided at all costs and even a small foray into it had left her suddenly weary again. She shut the book. 'Think I might try and get back to sleep again.'

Fletch nodded as she climbed back into her shell. 'Sure.' He pushed off the doorjamb. 'I've got some paperwork to get back to. I'll be in later.'

Just like old times.

Fletch waited another couple of hours and got into bed when she was asleep and that was pretty much the pattern for the following couple of weeks.

They went to bed at separate times, Tess first, he crawling in with her at some time after midnight, turning his back to her lest he do something crazy and reach for her because lying with her again, night after night, had been much harder than he'd ever suspected it would be.

Sure, there'd been other women since their divorce. Not many, but a few. They'd been brief episodes, a handful of dates, a slaking of a thirst more than anything, where he'd given in to the dictates of his body but had kept his heart well and truly out of the equation.

But he couldn't do that with Tess.

Lying in bed with her was a painful reminder of how good it had been between them back at a time where they'd been emotionally free to love each other. And in that strange twilight zone between sleep and waking it was easy to believe that nothing had changed between them.

His heart certainly thought so. After years of keeping it heavily guarded, it refused to buy into the happy-families façade. In those sleeping hours, when he had no conscious control, it knew her.

Knew Tess on a primal level.

Recognised the woman beside him as his mate.

It was only the slow dawning as he became more conscious that things got back under control. As each new day loomed ahead he remembered his place on the page. Days of her constant companionship, of smiling and laughing and pretending that things were fine. Of playing happy families.

No respite from her or the fears and failures of the past. No escape for his poor confused heart.

No escape from the fact that things weren't fine.

The embarrassing mornings didn't help. No matter how scrupulously they maintained distance as they drifted off to sleep, by morning their bodies had subconsciously sought the warmth and comfort neither of them would ask for consciously.

Fletch often woke spooned around her, an erection pressing into the soft cheeks of her bottom. Or on his stomach, one arm flung out, his hand spread possessively on her belly. Or on his side, snuggled up to her, his leg bent at the knee pinning her to the bed.

And then there were the times when he woke and

she was spooning him. Or had *her* hand on his belly. Or *her* leg entwined in his.

The only way to cope with their intimate postures had been to get up before her. Untangle himself and get out of the bedroom under the guise of taking Tabby outside for her morning toilet.

Do not stop. Do not look back.

And pretend it hadn't happened.

It certainly hadn't made for easy days despite outward appearances. The trepidation with which he greeted each day was tempered by Tess's academy-award-winning performance as chief organiser, but was there, nonetheless.

He knew it was difficult for her too yet she soldiered on, planning an activity every day to keep his mother, whose night-time wandering had settled dramatically, stimulated. Some days they cooked. Some days they rented classic movies that Jean knew well or visited some of Jean's old friends. Other times they went out to a museum or lunch in the city at a teahouse that had been around for a century.

His mother particularly enjoyed the morning and afternoon walks they took for Tabby's sake. Whether it was just Jean and Tess or he and his mother or the three of them, Jean chatted away happily as they trod the riverside boardwalk.

He knew his mother loved it when they were all together but frankly he preferred it when it was just the two of them. It felt forced with Tess there. Like they were trying too hard to be something that they weren't, that they hadn't been in a long time, that they could never be again, no matter how much their bodies betrayed them in their sleep.

And it felt...dishonest. Even if it was for a good cause.

And he knew she felt it too.

At the beginning of the third week there was a knock on the door as Fletch stacked the dishwasher after lunch. He'd not long got back from the hospital where the first patient in their study, a twenty-six-year-old motorbike accident victim, had been enrolled. 'I'll get it,' he said, waving off Tess who had put her sandwich down and risen from the table.

It was Trish. She was leaning against the door, looking huge and glowing at thirty weeks. Doug stood behind her, holding an excitable Christopher. Fletch's heart contracted at the sight of his nephew, at the features so familiar to him.

Trish kissed her brother's cheek. 'Okay,' she said, advancing into the apartment, 'I'm going stir crazy at home. The doc said I could have a little foray and your apartment was the only place that Doug would agree to take me to. Before you ask, all I've done is sit in a car and walk from my house to the car and from the car to your apartment.'

Fletch's lips twitched as Doug rolled his eyes. 'Okay, then.'

'Unc, unc, unc,' Christopher chanted, squirming in his father's arms, leaning forward and reaching out for Fletch. Just as Ryan had done when he'd come home from being at work for long hours. It was only natural for Fletch to take him and to plant a kiss on the baby-soft cheek.

'I'd kill for a cup of tea, which, by the way,' Trish said, smiling at him sweetly, 'you have to make because I'm not allowed to do anything.'

Fletch laughed. 'Well, come on in, then, and I'll make you one.'

Christopher still in tow, he entered the open lounge area, laughing at something Doug had said. It wasn't until he'd made it to the kitchen and heard an audible gasp that he realised the fuller implications.

He turned. Tess was frozen at the sink, her hands in sudsy water, staring at him. Or more correctly at Christopher.

He took a step towards her. 'Tessa.'

Tess held up her hands to stop him, suds sliding off them into the sink. The ache in her chest, the one that was always there, just smothered under years of pushing all the pain away, intensified.

The little boy in her ex-husband's arms smiled at her. A green-eyed little boy with blond hair that stuck up in the middle from his double cowlick.

A buzzing in her ears became so loud that for a moment she thought she was going to faint.

Ryan?

CHAPTER SIX

FLETCH handed Christopher back to his father. 'Tessa,' he said again, stepping towards her.

She backed up, her hip sliding along the bench. 'It's fine,' she said quickly, shaking her head. She didn't want him to touch her, to comfort her.

She just needed a moment.

There'd been other children in the last nine years. Of course there had been. Granted, they weren't common at the nursing home. But residents' grandchildren would come to visit and she'd coped. Smiled and agreed they were the most beautiful babies in the whole entire world and got on with her job.

But they were on the other side of the globe—not here.

Not in Fletch's arms.

Not looking like a carbon copy of Ryan.

She watched as the three adults looked at her, frozen in their positions, lost for words, waiting for her next move, not daring to even breathe in case she cracked into a thousand pieces. Only Christopher seemed oblivious, bouncing up and down in Doug's arms, making truck noises with his little bow lips.

Just as Ryan had done.

God, she was going to be sick.

'Excuse me for a moment, please,' she gasped as she whirled away from them and hurried to the main bathroom.

She lost her lunch and probably her breakfast too as she heaved into the toilet. A knock sounded on the door. 'Go away,' she yelled, knowing it would be Fletch.

Tears pricked at her eyes and she pressed her lids shut tight, beating them back. She'd cried her yearly allocation of tears at the cemetery a few weeks ago.

They were the boundaries she'd set herself and they'd worked for her.

And if she started now she might never stop.

After a few minutes Tess pulled herself up to sit on the closed lid, psyching herself up to go back out there. She had to do it, she knew that, but her cheeks warmed at the very thought. She'd completely and utterly embarrassed herself. Trish and Doug were guests in Fletch's home, not to mention family, and she'd made them feel uncomfortable.

And then, of course, there was Christopher…

Tess stood and looked at herself in the vanity mirror. She looked even whiter than her usual English pallor.

She looked like she'd seen a ghost.

She grimaced at the irony then turned on the tap, brushing her teeth and scrubbing vigorously at her face with cool water to put some colour back into her cheeks.

She dried off then inspected her face again. Marginally better.

'Go!' she ordered her reflection.

Thankfully her feet obeyed and Tess found herself walking out to join everyone, the thrum of her heartbeat in her ears. They had all joined Jean in the lounge area and were laughing at Christopher, who was patting Tabby.

Fletch, who wasn't really tuned in to the conversation, rose immediately when Tess came into his peripheral vision.

'You okay?' he asked anxiously.

Tess nodded as she drew closer. 'I'm sorry,' she apologised to Trish and Doug, whose attention was now also firmly on her. Thankfully, Jean was preoccupied with her grandson and Tabby. 'It was just a bit of a shock.'

Trish nodded. 'It's okay,' she assured gently. 'It really is quite freaky how similar they are.'

'No.' Tess shook her head. 'It's not okay. It was rude and I'm sorry.'

'Well, let's just agree to disagree on that one.' Fletch's sister grinned. 'Are you going to join us?' she asked.

Tess wanted to say no. To plead a headache or busy herself in the kitchen. But she'd already been unforgivably rude.

'It's fine if you don't want to,' Trish murmured.

'Don't be silly, Trish,' Jean said as her wandering attention came to rest on the byplay. She frowned at her daughter.

'Of course Tess wants to join us.' She patted the empty lounge next to her. 'Come and sit here, darling. Trish has brought one of the centre's little cherubs over for a visit.'

She squeezed Christopher's cheek and he squealed in delight then she looked at her daughter reproachfully. 'Trish, you know how much Tess adores children, why wouldn't she want to join us?'

Nobody said anything for a moment as Tess realised that Jean didn't have a clue that Christopher was her grandchild. Tess saw the flash of grief in Trish's eyes and noticed Doug's hand slide onto his wife's shoulder and squeeze.

'Of course I'll join you.' Tess smiled at Jean brightly.

Jean smiled back. 'Come and meet…oh, dear.' She turned to her daughter. 'What did you say his name was, Trish?'

Trish gave her mother a wan smile. 'Christopher, Mum.'

'Oh, what a gorgeous name.' Jean clapped her hands a few times. 'Maybe you can call this one…' she tapped Trish's belly '…Christopher if it's a boy? Tess?' She turned back to Tess. 'Did you know Trish was pregnant? You girls are so secretive these days!'

There was no need for a reply as Christopher's giggle distracted them all. Tabby was sniffing the toddler and her whiskers were buzzing the little boy's neck. He looked at his mother excitedly and said, 'Doggy!'

Trish laughed. 'Yes. Tabby. Can you say Tabby?'

Christopher gave another dribbly smile. 'Yabby, yabby, yabby!'

Everyone laughed then. Even Tess. Even though her heart ached just looking at Fletch's nephew.

After half an hour that stretched interminably Doug stood and announced it was time for a yawning Trish to go back to bed. Trish protested but Doug was firm. After a noisy round of goodbyes Jean and Fletch saw the trio to the door.

Tess watched them go, a lump rising in her throat as Christopher, who was grinning at her from over Doug's shoulder, waved madly at her. She'd spent the time they were there scrupulously not looking at him, not touching him, but there was just something about a happy, waving toddler that had her automatically waving back, even if she couldn't raise a corresponding smile.

Ryan had been such a friendly, easygoing little boy too.

It wasn't until she heard the door click closed that Tess finally relaxed.

Fletch crawled into bed just before midnight. It had been an eventful day. He'd tried to engage Tess in some conversation over his sister's unannounced visit but she'd insisted she was fine and didn't want to talk about it.

It was a touch too déjà vu for him but he'd learned ten years ago that Tess was hard to sway when her mind was made up. He lifted the sheet carefully and slowly lowered himself onto the mattress. He'd fallen into the habit of immediately turning his back on her but tonight, try as he may, he just couldn't. He propped himself up on his elbow and watched her for a while.

Her breathing was deep and steady but even in her sleep tonight her eyebrows seemed to be knitted in a frown. He wished he'd had the desire to confront her today about her avoidance issues. To say the things that needed to be said. That should have been said a decade ago.

But this wasn't a do-over of their marriage. This was her doing him a favour for a couple of months. He couldn't change what had happened back then in the aftermath of Ryan's death. The way grief had pushed them apart. And ultimately what he'd done when he'd been at emotional rock bottom.

There were so many things that had come between them. One heaping on top of the other until neither of them had been able to see the other any more.

And that wasn't going to be fixed by any enforced intimacy.

Fletch fell back against the pillows as a familiar rush

of disgust enveloped him, his actions that September night still haunting him.

But that too couldn't be changed.

He'd known it the second it had been done. And wishing it was different didn't make it so.

So he did what he'd done every night since she'd been back in his bed, what he'd done for so many nights after Ryan had died and she'd started shutting him out.

He rolled away from her and shut his eyes.

Tess woke to a wet feeling on her hand. Her eyes flew open as if they'd been zapped by a bolt of electricity. She backed up, accidentally nudging a prone Fletch as Tabby's dear old face filled her entire vision and the low, urgent whine went straight to a place deep and dark inside her.

Her heart beating like a runaway train, Tess's thoughts were incoherent for a moment or two.

It was Fletch who said, 'What is it, Tabby? Is Jean okay?' as he climbed out of bed.

Tess followed on autopilot. To Jean's room. The bed was empty. The bathroom—also empty. Then quickly out to the lounge. His laptop occupied the coffee table but there was no Jean. Around the dividing wall into the kitchen, where Jean was muttering to herself as she paced up and down.

Fletcher felt a rush of relief like a slug of tequila swamp him. 'Mum?'

Jean's hair was wild, like that of a mad scientist, as she looked at both of them with crazy eyes. 'Where's Ryan?' she demanded, her voice high with distress, her tone urgent. 'Tess? Where's Ryan? I thought I could hear him crying and I've searched the entire house but he's nowhere.' She put a hand to her mouth and her eyes grew large. 'What if he's been kidnapped?'

Whatever Tess had been expecting, it hadn't been this. She felt as if Jean had punched her in the stomach and she grabbed for the bench top to steady herself. Fletch had assured her that Jean didn't remember Ryan.

Just as she hadn't remembered poor little Christopher.

Tess didn't know what to say. Not after today. Not with Christopher's sweet little face such a poignant reminder of her own little boy. She could barely breathe, let alone form a coherent response.

'He's at Trish's,' Fletch said. 'Having a sleepover.'

Tess flinched as his hand came to rest on her shoulder, just as Doug's had done today with Trish.

'Trish wanted to give us a night off,' he embellished.

Jean seemed to sag as her agitation settled almost immediately. Tabby licked her hand and the transformation was complete. 'Well, why didn't you say so?' she accused mildly. 'I was worried half to death.'

Fletch flicked a glance at Tess. She still hadn't moved. Her distress wasn't as palpable as his mother's had been but he could tell she was rocked to the core. He wanted to go to her but his mother's needs were more immediate.

And a lot easier to fathom!

Jean patted her chest where the lacy yoke of her nightie met bare neck whilst she absently stroked Tabby with her other hand. 'That is so like Trish, though, isn't it?' She shook her head. 'I wish those two would stop wasting time and get pregnant. They'll make such great parents.'

Fletch nodded, his pulse settling. 'Would you like a warm milk, Mum?'

Jean gave him an indulgent smile, the missing Ryan already forgotten. 'That would be lovely, dear. Tess?'

Tess blinked. She could see Jean's lips moving but she couldn't hear any of the words. There was a pain in her chest, right in the centre of her heart, that was expanding rapidly and she could barely breathe.

'Tess?'

Fletch's deep grumbly voice pierced her inertia. She looked at him. What did he want? What had he said?

'Milk?' he prompted in response to her blank look.

Tess shook her head as the pain became a pressure that built relentlessly. Pushing against her rib cage, clogging her throat, pressing against the backs of her eyes.

She couldn't stay here. And drink milk. She couldn't pretend that her mother-in-law's state tonight hadn't affected her. It may have sprung from Jean's confused condition but to her anything to do with Ryan was absolutely crystal clear.

And sometimes still so very real.

No matter how much she tried to ignore it.

'Tess?' Fletch prompted again, laying his palm over hers.

She pulled away. 'No.' She shook her head. 'Thanks,' she added. 'I think I'm just going to go back to bed. It's late...'

Fletch nodded. 'Of course.' He searched her face, her amber eyes looking huge in her thin, haunted face. 'I'll be in later,' he murmured.

But he doubted she'd heard him as he spoke the words to her retreating back.

Tess lay in the dark, staring at the ceiling, while her body waged a war between sleep and grief. She wanted to sleep. She wanted to be able to shut her eyes and let a black tide wash her away into the embrace of a deep, dreamless slumber. And she wanted to be there before Fletch came back to bed.

But memories of Ryan—memories she'd spent a decade suppressing—refused to be quelled and swept her along on another black tide. A rough-and-tumble ride that left her feeling bruised and battered.

The way his hair had smelled. His delighted little giggle. His fat pudgy fingers that had wound into her hair as he'd sucked his thumb. His father's silver-green eyes that had lit with mischief or wonder. The way every single discovery had been met with complete awe. The way he'd looked up at her as he'd fed at her breast, with such unconditional love and trust.

Trust that she had destroyed completely as she'd slept that morning ten years ago while her son had drowned.

'Tess?' Fletch approached the bed tentatively half an hour later. His mother was settled back in bed with Tabby, blissfully unaware of the emotional carnage she'd left in her wake. 'Tess?' he said again.

The room was dark and her back was to the door but he knew she was awake. He could sense her turmoil as if it had flashed out at him like a lighthouse beacon.

'I'm sorry, Tess. She hasn't mentioned Ryan in well over a year. It was probably having Christopher here today that triggered latent memories.'

He climbed into bed beside her, sitting up with his back against the headboard. Her shoulder was bare and his fingers itched to touch it. To loan her some comfort.

To seek some comfort.

But he couldn't bear her to flinch at his touch again. 'Tess?'

Tess, her eyes squeezed tight, contemplated continuing to ignore him but it was patently obvious he hadn't bought into her act. She opened her eyes on a huffed-out breath. She rolled onto her back. 'It's fine, Fletch. Go to sleep.'

He looked down at her, her amber gaze glimmering with unshed tears and tightly reined emotions. 'I can't.'

Her eyes, accustomed to the dark, watched him for a moment or two. He looked like someone had knocked the stuffing out of him and she realised that Jean's out-burst hadn't been easy for him either. Both the distress-ing state of her and the subject matter.

She pushed herself up to sit beside him, ensuring there was a decent distance between them, and they sat contemplating the darkness around them for a few moments.

'I'm sorry,' Tess murmured. 'It was… I got a bit of a shock when Jean said… I wasn't expecting it.'

Fletch nodded. 'I know.'

They fell quiet again. 'I miss him,' he said eventually.

Tess squeezed her eyes shut again as the pressure spiked behind her eyeballs. 'Don't, Fletch.'

'He loved her, though, didn't he, my mum? Do you remember how he used to call her Ninny?' He laughed. 'And she used to call him Rinny?'

Tess drew her knees up and shook her head. She didn't want to be sucked back into those days. When their lives had been perfect and nothing had been able to touch them. The pressure became unbearable. 'Fletch.'

Fletch heard the note of warning in her voice under-pinned by a tautness that could have strung piano wire. He shoved a hand through his hair. 'Damn it, Tessa, I'm so sick of not talking about him…of not having any-one to talk about him to. Surely after ten years we can reminisce without it being so…fraught?'

His voice may have been low and husky but to Tess it sounded like a clanging gong in the silence, and the dam holding back her grief started to crack.

Fletch turned to implore her. He just wanted to remember his son for a few minutes with the one person who had loved him with the same intensity and devotion.

Couldn't she give him that at least?

He noticed her hands trembling first against her drawn-up thighs. Then her shoulders shaking. Then a low noise, like a wounded animal. 'Tessa?'

Tess shut her eyes on a sob that broke free from her throat. A tear squeezed out. Then another.

Fletch felt as if a giant hand had grabbed a big loop of his intestine and twisted—hard. Why hadn't he just kept his big trap shut? 'Tess?'

She couldn't respond. Couldn't talk. Daren't open her mouth for fear all her locked-in grief would come spewing out and she'd never survive the fallout.

He turned on his side, reaching out a hand, touching her shoulder, waiting for the flinch, determined this time to push through it and comfort her. But there was only more sobbing.

Not great honking sobs either. Pitiful, muted ones.

Apportioned. Rationed. Kept strictly under control.

But he knew what they'd cost her.

When she'd announced two months after Ryan's death there'd be no tears, she'd been true to her word.

Still, he hadn't meant to upset her. He'd just needed…

What? What had he needed?

Connection.

'I'm sorry,' he murmured, scooting closer. 'God, Tess don't…please.'

He pushed his hands into her hair and swiped at her tears with his thumbs. 'Shh, it's okay, honey, don't.'

Even though he knew if anyone needed to cry it was Tess, her pathetic mewing was so heart-wrenching he couldn't bear it. He leaned in and kissed her forehead. Kissed her eyelids. His lips mingled with her tears. 'Shh,' he crooned as he tasted both their salt and their anguish.

His palms moved down to cradle her face as he followed the tracks of her tears, sipping at them as he went. Down the slopes of her prominent cheekbones. Into the dip of the hollows beneath. Past her nose. To the corner of her mouth.

'Shh,' he murmured against her lips. 'Shh.'

And then the soft butterfly presses became something else. Something different.

Something more.

Tess felt her wretchedness ease as something altogether took over. Something unusual yet familiar. Hesitant yet insistent.

Something separate from her grief.

And she grabbed on for dear life.

Her mouth opened beneath his and the harsh suck of his breath echoed around them. Her tongue reached out tentatively, seeking his, and she felt his deep groan reach right down inside her to places she'd long since forgotten existed.

Places that were coming to life with a roar, not a whimper. Heating and liquefying and pulsating.

Fletch's hand slid from her jaw to the back of her head, angling it so he could deepen the kiss. Tess obliged, letting him in a little more, sighing against his mouth. He slid his hand to her back, gathering her closer, their chests touching, their hips aligned, their legs brushing.

She wound her arms around his neck, the motion squashing her breasts against his chest, and Fletch could feel their softness and the twin points of her aroused nipples that told him more than her sigh ever could.

His head spun, his pulse tripped. Her lips tasted sweet and every time he drew in a breath the aroma of Tess, imprinted on his DNA, filled up his senses.

It was intoxicating. She was intoxicating. And it had been *so damn long*.

He didn't know what was going on but right now he couldn't have cared less. All he knew was that he needed this, needed her, with a gnawing, aching desperation.

Tess could feel her body igniting. From the sealed heat of their mouths, liquid warmth oozed like quicksilver into her marrow. Into every muscle and sinew. Into every cell. Pushing forth into areas that had been shut down for a decade. Where she'd felt cold and bleak for a decade.

She felt Fletch's hand at her breast and she moaned into his mouth, arching her back, pushing herself harder into his palm, her hips moving more intimately against his. She felt the thickness of his arousal and rocked herself into it. The guttural sound he made at the back of his throat fuelled the flames licking through her blood and the urgent hand he clamped against her bottom, where cheek met thigh, pressed her closer. She had no idea what she was doing. All she knew was it felt good. And in the storm of sensations she'd found a new way to reach the oblivion she craved.

Respite from thoughts of Ryan that had been hammering at her skull ever since Jean's clueless ramblings.

Suddenly she wasn't a grieving mother or a failed wife. She was a woman. And she felt whole again.

Whole.

The word was like a glacial hand on her neck and Tess froze in his arms. Since when had she needed a man to feel whole?

Especially this man, whom she'd loved too much and knew too well?

She'd moved to the other side of the world to get away from him, to get the emotional distance she'd needed just to survive. And she hadn't so much as looked at a man in a decade. Yet one touch from Fletch and she was practically climbing on top of him?

Undoing all the hard work. Knocking down all the emotional barriers she'd erected to survive in a world that had been turned upside down.

What was she doing?

She couldn't need Fletch to feel whole again. She just couldn't. She had a life to go back to. A life that worked.

A life without him.

She wasn't here for this. She didn't want this.

She didn't need it.

Fletch realised suddenly that Tess had stopped responding. He drew back, his heart racing, his breath ragged. 'Tess?'

She could see desire turning his silvery-green eyes all smoky. Her chest rose and fell in the same agitated rhythm as his. She pushed against him. 'Let me go.'

Fletch blinked. *Huh?*

She pushed harder. 'I can't do this. Let me go,' she said, more frantic this time.

Fletch felt like the bed had been yanked out from under him as she wrenched away. 'Tess. No.' He grabbed for her but she'd removed herself from the arc of his reach.

She shook her head as she scrambled to the farthest point of the bed from him, her back against the headboard again. She yanked her oversized shirt down over her drawn-up knees until only the tips of her toes were visible.

As a physical deterrent it was fairly flimsy but symbolically it screamed *Keep out* very effectively. She hunched into it. 'I'm sorry,' she whispered. 'I can't.'

Fletch fell back against the mattress, suppressing a roar of frustration. His pulse hammered, his breath rasped, his erection strained.

'It's fine,' he said after a few moments, staring at the ceiling.

Even though it wasn't. Even though déjà vu was pressing him into the mattress with the weight of a hundred bitter memories. Reaching out for her on too many occasions and being rebuffed. Desperate to hold her, to reaffirm their love, all met with stony resistance.

And whilst she may not have flinched away this time, her sudden change of mind was just as gutting. Because for the first time in a decade she'd needed him.

He'd never been surer of anything.

She'd needed him.

'I don't know what happened,' Tess said.

Fletch's obvious wretchedness added guilt to the mix of her ricocheting emotions. The need to explain herself took her by surprise.

Fletch shut his eyes. 'It's fine,' he dismissed again.

But it wasn't. She didn't want him to think she was playing games. 'I haven't… I don't… It just…took me away. Before I knew it, nothing else existed.'

Fletch shoved a hand through his hair as her meaning sank in and he felt cold all over. So she *had* needed him.

As a distraction.

A sudden surge of anger boiled away the ice.

She'd used him.

Tess realised what she'd said as he rolled out of bed. 'Wait, Fletch…I didn't mean… It's not like that…'

Fletch looked across the rumpled bed at her, anger simmering in his veins. 'Yes, it is, Tess,' he said quietly, his jaw locked tight, keeping rigid control of his response. 'It's exactly like that.'

And before he could say something he regretted, he did what he'd always done, turned away and walked out of the room.

CHAPTER SEVEN

Tess lay awake long after Fletch had left, staring into the darkness. He didn't come back to bed and she knew in her bones he wouldn't. She fell asleep as dawn was breaking across a velvet sky and didn't wake until the sun was high.

Even then she couldn't move. She just lay on her side and watched a vapour trail leave a white streak across the slice of sky she could see through the bedroom's large windows, her thoughts full of Fletch.

And their kiss.

It was time to admit to herself that living in such close quarters with him had loosened the lid on feelings she'd thought long suppressed.

She was attracted to Fletch.

It was simply undeniable. It had been there from the first moment she'd spotted him at the cemetery. Fletch had improved with age and there was a sexiness to his maturity that pulled at her in places entirely different from those the first time around.

And to someone who hadn't felt attraction or desire in such a long time, *who'd actually shunned it*, it wasn't an easy admission.

It was made worse by the answering flicker she'd seen in him. From the moment he'd looked at her bare thighs that first night to the way she'd caught him looking at her in unguarded moments, it was obvious he felt it too.

It had been wrong of her, stupid actually, to think they could just pick up where they'd left off—two human beings going through the motions, shells of what they'd once been—with this attraction raging between them.

But she hadn't meant to use him.

It had just been so good to forget for a while after Jean's unintended stirring-up of their past.

Her stomach muscles tightened as the kiss played in her head again and for a fleeting moment Tess regretted pushing him away last night. Maybe she should have just got lost in him, like she used to. Let him and the magic she knew their bodies could make obliterate everything.

The time between going to bed and falling asleep was always the hardest—last night particularly—and he could have helped with that.

But she just…couldn't.

She'd known she was getting herself into dangerous emotional waters, a torrent she'd barely survived the last time, and she just hadn't been able to let go.

Her life was too regimented for that.

She'd tried to live her life simply and on a level emotional plane ever since they'd separated. She'd moved far away and started anew. She lived modestly, kept friendships light, actively discouraged men. She worked and she slept and in between times she kept herself busy in her garden or doing online research for the local historical society.

She didn't even have a pet.

Jumping head first into a sexual liaison with Fletch

as a way to keep the memories at bay during her stint in his apartment was a huge leap and one that was pure folly. Pretending they were happily married for Jean's sake was enough of a lie without throwing sex into the mix.

Because even she knew with their history and this latent attraction, it could never be that simple.

And she didn't want to need Fletch again like she once had. Ten years of separation had afforded her a true sense of self. She didn't need anybody these days and that was fine and dandy as far as she was concerned.

Because when she was done here she *was* going back to England, back to her perfectly fine life in a small Devonshire village where everyone knew her name and no one knew her pain.

Just the way she liked it.

But first she had to get through the next weeks and to do that she had to get out of bed and go and talk to Fletch.

Fletch squinted against the harsh morning sunshine reflecting off the river as he stood at the railing of his deck. He and his mother had just come back from taking Tabby for a walk along the river path he could see snaking down below.

He took a long swallow of the ice-cold berry smoothie they'd whipped up together on their return. Tess had stocked the freezer with frozen berries, quoting something about their antioxidant properties being good for Jean's memory retention.

He was pretty sure it wouldn't stand up to any rigorous scientific testing but the nutritional value of berries was well documented and blended with ice and a little cream they went down very well on a hot morning.

He yawned as his lack of sleep caught up with him. His neck ached from hunching over the laptop at the coffee table, pretending to work, while his brain had turned the incident with Tess over and over until he'd thought he was going to pass out from the spinning.

He'd been angry with Tess when he'd walked out on her last night. And it hadn't been from some thwarted sexual fulfilment. Or the fact that she had been using him to forget for a while.

Well, not entirely anyway.

It was her rejection of his closeness, her continual refusal to let him in, to talk to him, that had steam blowing out of his ears.

It was déjà vu.

By the time his mother had woken at seven he had been angry with himself. For a start, he'd been foolish to believe he could just share a bed with Tess and not want to get her naked. Despite their history he was still dangerously attracted to her and he'd known that from the first night when she'd put her hand on his thigh.

Secondly, he was angry because he should have never given up on her.

On them.

He should have insisted on counselling instead of the gently-gently approach he'd taken. Demanded she come with him. Picked her up and carried her there if necessary.

Maybe they'd still be together.

He should have said no when she'd asked for the divorce.

But things had been so dark and bleak for so long and he'd just done something utterly and completely unconscionable. Sure, there had been a thousand excuses and justifications but he hadn't believed any of them then and the passage of time hadn't made them any more palatable.

It had been too hard to look at her, and impossible to look at himself.

And she'd given him the perfect out.

Walking away had been the only option. Because telling her hadn't been.

Just as starting something with her while she was here wasn't an option either. Not with so much unsaid between them.

Fletch drained his glass and moved inside, his eyes instantly grateful. His mother was washing up at the sink and she smiled at him as he placed his glass into the soapy water and picked up a tea towel.

'Tess on an early today?' she asked.

Fletch shook his head as he'd done the last six times she'd asked. 'She's on a day off. She's having a lie-in.'

It had been hard for him, watching his mother's memory slowly regress. Worse for Trish who had done more of the hands-on caring over the last couple of years. That she'd remembered Ryan last night had been completely unexpected. And if she'd been in her right mind Fletch knew his mother would have been mortified by what she'd said.

He wished he knew what was going on inside her head. He wished he knew so he could fix it. But there were just some things that couldn't be fixed.

He knew that better than most.

He turned to put the glasses away in the cupboards behind him and he smiled at the little sticker that had a picture of a tumbler and had *glasses* written in neat black print. Thanks to Tess, nearly every single surface in his apartment bore labels—cupboards, light switches, electrical appliances. Her handiwork was everywhere.

She was everywhere.

In a short space of time she'd made such a huge difference—cupboards and drawers had symbols on them, labels above power points reminded Jean to turn the power off when she was finished with it. Tess had added to the book that Trish had instigated containing basic but important information like name, age, address, appointments, etc. A map and directions back to home had been included and Tess wrote in it each day what they were going to do so it had become a communication tool as well.

She'd bought Jean a journal and encouraged her to write down her thoughts and ideas, to use the book each day as a way to keep her mind exercised. She'd even made an appointment for Fletch at the family lawyer to review and update the legal and financial documents that he and Trish and Jean had put into place five years ago when his mother had first been diagnosed with Alzheimer's.

And then, of course, there was the dog.

There was no doubt about it—Tess had made herself indispensable. And his mother was more settled, more content than he'd seen her in a long time.

But her presence was a double-edged sword.

It reminded him of what he'd had. What had happened.

And how badly he'd screwed up.

Tess took some deep, cleansing breaths as she walked down the hallway to the lounge area. She could hear the clinking of dishes and Fletch and Jean chatting as she grew nearer, and it felt so domestic she wondered if she hadn't been caught in some kind of bizarre time warp.

The urge to pack up her things and return to her isolation on the other side of the world grew with each footstep closer. But she'd told Fletch she'd stay until after Trish's baby was born and she wouldn't go back on her word.

Fletch looked up as Tess appeared in the kitchen. She was wearing above-the-knee denim cut-offs and a tank top. Her hair was damp and spiky, her feet were bare and she wore no make-up.

She looked utterly gorgeous. A soothing sight for tired eyes. A decade ago he would have teased her about sleeping in. Hell, a decade ago he would have been right in bed beside her.

But their kiss from last night stood large between them and he gave her a polite smile instead. 'Morning,' he murmured. She gave a wan nod in reply.

'Tess, don't you have an early today?' Jean asked as she squeezed out the dishcloth.

Tess shook her head. 'Not today.'

Fletch watched as she stood there looking awkward. 'Berry smoothie?' he asked.

She nodded. 'I can get it.'

Fletch was already halfway to the fridge. 'It's fine,' he dismissed. 'Why don't you go out to the deck and I'll bring it out to you?'

Tess acquiesced. She figured it was best to get the inevitable out of the way and try and move forward from the awkwardness of last night.

Bright sunshine enveloped her as she stepped outside and headed straight for the railing. She shut her eyes and turned her pale face to the source of the heat, revelling in it as if she were an unfurling flower. The hit of UV was so intoxicating she didn't hear Fletch approach a few moments later.

Fletch was engrossed by the image before him. Tess on his deck, her face raised to the sun in silent supplication. He wanted to stroke the ice-cold glass down her bare arm, drop a kiss against her nape. What had happened last night had changed things between them and despite her rejection of him, he still wanted to touch her.

'Here,' he murmured, holding out the glass to her from a safe distance.

Tess opened her eyes reluctantly. She'd forgotten how good it felt to be deep-down-in-your-bones warm. 'Thank you,' she said, taking the offering but avoiding his gaze.

Fletch took up position beside her but not too close. He leaned heavily against the rail, waiting for her to take a couple of sips before he said what he'd come out to say. 'I owe you an apology over last night.'

Tess shook her head, her gaze fixed on the river below. 'It's okay, Fletch.'

'No, it's not. I was rude.'

She shrugged. 'You were right.'

Fletch glanced at her sharply. He hadn't expected her to say that.

'I *was* using you,' she said, her eyes fixed on the wide expanse of the water below. 'Not intentionally... but deep down...'

Fletch looked at her for a long moment before glancing at the view below. Her candour vindicated him but it didn't make him feel any better. 'I'm sorry things got so out of hand, Tess. I wouldn't blame you if you wanted to turn tail and run.'

Tess looked up for the first time. 'I told you I'd stay until after Trish has the baby and I will.'

He glanced at her again and their gazes meshed. 'Thank you.'

Tess nodded. He looked so serious. So different from the smoky-eyed lover of last night.

'I was thinking…' he said. 'Mum seems settled now with Tabby for company. Maybe I should go back to the couch?'

Tess regarded him for a moment then looked away. It was a sensible suggestion, given what had happened, but this thing wasn't about them. It was about Jean.

'She's still wandering, Fletch.'

'Not very often.'

'Yes, but you know how upset she became that night when she thought you and I were going to get divorced. I don't know about you, but I don't want her to have to go through that again—it's not good for her or her blood pressure. Actually…' Tess thought back to her own response to the distressing incident. 'It's not good for any of us.'

Fletch nodded. He knew what she was saying was right.

But…

'It would make things easier for us,' he pointed out.

Or him anyway. Sharing a bed with her had been hard enough without last night's little session playing like an erotic movie on slow-mo through his head.

And now he'd tasted her again? And realised he was as hot for her as he ever was? He wasn't sure he was capable of waking tangled up in her and not letting his natural urges take over.

Tess looked at him. 'It's not about us, Fletch.'

Fletch met her calm amber gaze. She was right, of

course. But he wasn't so sure he could compartmental-
ise it as easily as she had.

She'd always been the expert in that department.

A few nights later Tess was woken again in the wee
hours. Fortunately this time it was Fletch's pager and
not his mother.

It had been a long time since she'd been woken by
a pager. When they'd been married it had been a regu-
lar occurrence that had barely caused her to stir but all
these years later it was disorientating for a moment.

'What's that noise?' Tess murmured as she groped
through layers of sleep. The soft pillow beneath her head
was warm and pliant and she snuggled into it farther.

Fletch was instantly awake. Tess's head was on his
shoulder, her body curled into his, her hand on his belly
dangerously close to a piece of his anatomy that had
obviously been up for a while. 'Shh, it's okay,' he murmured. 'It's just my pager. Go back to sleep.'

He gently eased away from her as he reached for
his pager, dislodging her hand and her head and her
thigh crossed over his at the knee. He wished it was as
easy to remove the lingering aroma of her hair in his
nostrils and the warm imprint of her body against his.
He pushed a button on the device and read the backlit screen.

Displaced, Tess roused further. She frowned. 'You
have a pager?'

'I'm on call for the study,' he explained quietly as
he swung his legs over the side of the bed and his feet
hit the floor. 'They need me to consent an admission.
There's no one on that can do it.'

Only certain medical and nursing staff that'd done
in-service on the study had been cleared to give consent.

A large percentage of the staff across the two units had been trained up to ensure there was always someone on shift who could do it but occasionally it worked out that some shifts just weren't covered.

Tess yawned, her heavy eyes refusing to open. 'What time is it?' she asked as she tried to snuggle into her actual pillow, finding it nowhere near as comfortable.

'Two-thirty,' Fletch whispered as he stood. 'Go to sleep.'

No answer was forthcoming and he turned to look at her. She had taken his advice. The urge to lean over and drop a goodbye kiss on her mouth surprised him with its intensity. It was certainly what he would have done had they still been married.

But they weren't.

Twenty minutes later Fletch was walking into the PICU at St Rita's. He'd pulled on some jeans, thrown on a T-shirt, stuffed his feet into a pair of joggers and finger-combed his hair. He'd quickly brushed his teeth and ignored the fact that he needed a shave.

Time was of the essence where head injuries were concerned.

Every female staff member on the unit practically swooned as he entered. Any distraction from weariness was welcome at three a.m. and Fletch's particular brand of scruffy chic especially so.

'What have we got?' he asked Dr Joella Seaton, the registrar covering the night shift.

'Kyle Drayson. Eighteen-month-old immersion retrieved from Toowoomba area.'

She handed Fletch the chart and continued, unaware that Fletch had stopped listening.

'Incident occurred at a local swimming hole where

the family were camping at just after midnight. He'd woken and wandered away from the camp site. Local ambulance arrived within twenty minutes of call. After an extended down time they got a rhythm. He was medivaced out. He's not quite three hours post-injury.'

Joella stopped talking and waited for Fletch to say something. He blinked when he realised they were standing outside room two and he hadn't been aware they'd been walking.

Of course. *Room two.*

'Dr King?'

Fletch looked blankly at Joella. What had she said? 'I'm sorry, Joella, go on.'

'Mum came in the chopper with him. She's obviously very distressed. She's currently with the on-call social worker.'

Fletch nodded as his demons prowled in front of the closed double doors. A glass window allowed him to see some of the activity as nurses scurried about, trying to stabilise the patient.

An eighteen-month-old patient. Who had nearly drowned.

Not a forty-year-old motorcyclist who'd been going too fast around a bend. Or a nineteen-year-old skateboarder who hadn't wanted to look uncool in a helmet. Or a sixty-year-old golfer who'd been smacked in the head with a flying ball.

A boy. A little boy.

And he had to go into the room. He had to go in and stand at the end of bed two and look at little Kyle who had nearly drowned. Just as he'd done with Ryan ten years ago.

As a doctor this time, not a father.

For a moment he doubted he could. Not this room. Not another eighteen-month-old boy.

His pulse roared in his ears. His gut felt as if it had tied itself into the mother of all knots. Right now he would have paid Joella every cent he owned not to.

But he believed in this study. He believed in therapeutic hypothermia for acute brain injury. Had seen over and over how neuro-protective decreasing a patient's body temperature could be. How it could reduce the harmful effects of ischemia by reducing the rate of cellular metabolism and therefore the body's need for oxygen. How it stabilised cell membranes. How it moderated intracranial pressure.

He believed he could give Kyle and kids like him—*kids like Ryan*—a better neurological outcome with a simple non-invasive therapy.

And to do that, he had to do his job.

He had to walk into room two and be a doctor.

Tess was getting back into bed from her dash to the loo when Fletch entered the bedroom a couple of hours after he'd left. She glanced at the clock. Four-thirty. There was a moment of awkwardness as their eyes briefly met but his gaze slipped quickly away and he barely acknowledged her before he headed for the bathroom.

'Did you get your consent?' she asked his back as it disappeared. She pulled the sheet up as the light went on in the bathroom. He didn't answer. In fact, she wasn't even sure he'd heard her.

'Yes.'

Tess turned her head towards the bathroom and for a brief moment caught his backlit haggard face before he snapped the light off.

She stifled a gasp. He looked like he'd aged ten years in a couple of hours.

Drawn, pinched, tense.

Old.

He looked like he had that day with Ryan.

She sat up. 'Are you okay?'

Fletch sank down on his side of the bed, his back to her. He shut his eyes for a moment, rubbed a hand through his hair. Kyle Drayson's face, his blond hair and green eyes so like Ryan's, seemed to be tattooed on the insides of his eyelids. He opened them, lifted the sheet and slipped under it.

'I'm fine,' he said, conscious of her face peering down at him.

Tess may have spent nine years apart from Fletch but she still knew him well enough to know that he wasn't fine. Knew that whatever he'd gone to see at work hadn't been pretty. She'd worked in ICU. She remembered too well those times when it was even too much for seasoned veterans.

And she'd been on the other side of the bed too. So had Fletch. Except he was still there, at the coal face.

How did he do it?

'Was it bad?'

Fletch sighed. 'I'm fine,' he repeated.

His voice was telling her to leave it alone but his utter wretchedness provoked her to push. 'Was it the kids or the adults?'

'The PICU.'

His terse reply put an itch up her spine. 'Do you… want to talk about it?'

Fletch shut his eyes. He wanted to do anything but. He wanted to be able to get in a time machine and erase the last few hours. He wanted to go back and stop Kyle from leaving his tent. Or further still. Stop Ryan from leaving the lounge room via a door Tess had been nagging him to fix.

'It might help,' she murmured, looking down into his tense face, his forehead scrunched, his lips flattened.

He snorted, his eyes flying open. 'Oh, and you would know that how?'

How many times had he begged her to talk to him?

Tess blinked at the flash of venom reflecting like a great orb in his silvery-green gaze. He was right. Psychological advice coming from her was hypocritical in the extreme. But something was very obviously wrong.

And she couldn't bear to see him so troubled.

She'd been blind to his torment a decade ago but she could see it with absolute clarity now.

'Forget it,' he said, flicking the covers back and vaulting upright. He swung his legs over the edge of the bed.

Tess frowned at the expanse of his back. 'Fletch?' She reached out a tentative hand and touched his shoulder. He flinched and her hand fell away. The rejection stung.

Fletch buried his face in his hands for a few moments, the spike of rage dissipating as fast as it had arrived. His hands dropped into his lap and his shoulders sagged. 'I'm sorry.'

Tess watched him for a moment, feeling utterly impotent in the face of his turmoil. She wished she had some words for him but she was at a loss.

'It was a little boy. Blond hair. Green eyes. Eighteen months old. An immersion. They'd put him in room two.'

The words fell like stones—like huge boulders, actually—into the silence. If Tess thought she'd been lost for words before, she was practically rendered mute now.

There were no words.

So she did the only thing she could think of. The only thing that felt right. She reached for his shoulder again. This time he didn't flinch. This time he covered her hand with one of his own.

She moved closer then. Parted her legs so his back fitted into her front, his bottom pressed into the place where her thighs joined, her legs bracketing his. She pressed her cheek against his T-shirt just below his shoulder blade. It smelled of detergent and sunshine and man.

She felt and heard the steady thump of his heartbeat. Found comfort in its slow, assured pulse.

She wasn't sure how long they sat there. All she knew was that when she whispered, 'Come on,' to him, he let her pull him back, let her draw him down until his head was resting on her chest, his ear over her own heartbeat, her arm around his shoulders.

'What's his name?' she asked after a while.

'Kyle.'

Tess ran the name around in her head for a moment. 'Did they give consent? His parents? For your study?'

Fletch nodded. 'The mother did.'

And because neither of them wanted to talk about Kyle or Ryan, she stroked his hair and asked him about the medicine. The medicine was safe. It was clinical. Unemotional. Free of baggage.

'Was he part of the treatment group or the control?'

'Treatment,' Fletch confirmed. 'They had the cooling blanket beneath him and were actively cooling him when I left.'

'What's the goal, temperature-wise?'

'We only want to induce moderate hypothermia for forty-eight hours.'

Tess shivered at the thought. She knew that freezing water would currently be running through the latex underblanket and that Kyle's skin would be icy to touch in a matter of hours. He would be oblivious, kept in an induced coma, but still the thought gave her chills and she was grateful for the heat of Fletch and his big arm encircling her waist.

'That's different from your earlier studies,' she murmured.

He turned his head to look up at her. 'You've read my studies?'

Tess allowed a ghost of a smile to touch her lips. 'I've read all your published stuff.'

Fletch was speechless for a moment. A hundred things to say crowded to his lips but he dismissed them all. He'd often wondered if she'd ever thought of him.

It was good to know she had.

Tess let him talk. Listened to the rumble of his voice as he told her about his earlier studies. About his experiences in Canada with cold-water immersions having better neurological outcomes than those he'd seen in Australia. How because of Ryan he'd developed a special interest in the subject, which had fast developed into an obsession.

And somehow hearing her son's name when they were both wrapped up together, keeping their demons at bay, didn't seem so gut-wrenching.

The irony of it all wasn't lost on her. Not even at five in the morning after another disrupted night.

Why had it taken her ten years to comfort him?

This was what he'd needed, what he'd asked for so

many times in so many ways, and she'd denied him because she just hadn't been capable.

When he'd needed her most, she'd pushed him away.

She should have been there for him more.

She'd failed Fletch as well as Ryan.

CHAPTER EIGHT

Two weeks later Tess was in the middle of a lesson in making royal icing flowers when the phone rang. She reached across to the nearby wall where it was hanging and plucked it off the cradle, all without taking her eyes off the deft precision of Jean's wrinkled fingers as they created sweet perfection.

Tabby lay at their feet, ready for any morsel that inadvertently landed on the floor, and Tess absently stroked the dog's back with her foot as she said, 'Tess speaking.'

Jean held up a perfectly formed miniature rose for her approval and Tess grinned and silently applauded.

'Oh...hi, it's Trish. How are you?'

Tess heard the disappointment in her ex-sister-in-law's voice. She'd spoken to Trish a few times on the phone since the day they'd turned up with Christopher, just a quick hello and goodbye as she'd handed the phone to Jean or Fletch. But she knew that Trish rang religiously every day to speak to her mother.

'You want to talk to Jean?'

'No. I was hoping to speak to Fletch, actually. Is he there?'

Tess shook her head, even though Trish couldn't see her. 'He's at the hospital at the moment.'

'Oh…do you know when he'll be home?'

There was more than disappointment in Trish's voice. There was something else. Worry?

'Not till about five. They've had quite a few study enrolments the last couple of weeks so he's got a bit to catch up on.'

'Right. Damn it.'

'Is there something wrong, Trish?'

'I was hoping he could watch Christopher for me for a couple of hours. I have an appointment for my thirty-two-week scan. Normally I'd take Christopher but he's unwell at the moment. Doctor says it's a virus, but he's totally miserable so I don't want to drag him from pillar to post. And I can't leave a sick child with any of my friends—they all have kids. It's fine, Doug will just have to stay home and look after him instead of coming to the scan with me.'

Tess remembered how Fletch had been there at all her scans. How he'd revelled in the experience as much as she had. How it had bonded them even closer when they'd been able to share the images of their unborn son together, watch his little heart beat, his perfect little limbs kicking away like crazy.

'What about Doug's mother?' Tess asked.

'She's up north, visiting relatives.'

And they both knew Jean wasn't capable. 'Could you reschedule?'

'They've already squeezed me in on a cancellation. My obstetrician is always booked to the eyeballs.'

Tess felt an encroaching dread as she contemplated the right thing to do. Back in the old days she wouldn't have hesitated to offer her services. But the mere thought of looking after Christopher terrified her.

'Doug won't mind,' Trish assured her. 'He's pretty easygoing.'

Tess hated the awkwardness between them now. That Trish wasn't even asking her. That she was obviously trying to reassure her. Once upon a time Trish would have just asked, secure in the knowledge that Tess would say yes.

She shut her eyes, knowing she couldn't let Doug miss out on this experience when she was perfectly capable of looking after a small child. 'I...I can do it.'

Her voice quavered, her heart pounded, but she'd offered.

Silence greeted her from the other end. Then, 'Oh, Tess... It's fine, you don't have to do that...'

Tess shook her head. 'Doug shouldn't miss out on this, Trish.' More silence. 'Of course I'd understand if you preferred I didn't.'

There was silence on the other end again for a long time and Tess wondered if Trish had hung up. *God, Trish really didn't want her looking after Christopher.* And as much as she didn't want to do it either, it hurt.

'Look, it doesn't matter,' Tess said, gripping the phone hard. 'It was just a thought. Forget it. I know my track record's not...'

She couldn't finish. She couldn't say that the last little boy she'd been left in charge of had drowned.

'What? Oh, Tess, no! I'm sorry, I was just thinking. Christopher doesn't really know you, that's all. It's not about... I didn't mean to...'

Trish fell silent and Tess heard a long, deep sigh.

'I don't blame you, Tess...for what happened to Ryan.' Trish's voice was husky with sincerity. 'No one has ever blamed you. Not Mum. Not me or Doug. And certainly not Fletch.'

'I know.'

And she did know. But what Trish and Jean and Fletch didn't realise was that no matter what they thought, no matter how much time passed, she would *always* blame herself.

'I would very much appreciate it if you could watch Christopher for me, Tess. It would be a big help.'

Tess felt a thunk in her chest and had the insane urge to take the offer back. But it was out there now and Trish's voice was suddenly unburdened of the worry and disappointment that had been present at the beginning of the conversation.

And it meant something that Trish had faith in her.

'What time's the appointment?' she asked.

'In an hour. Do you mind me asking if you and Mum could come here? He's asleep now and I'm pretty sure he's going to be out to it for the afternoon—I'd rather not disturb him. Tell you what, why don't I take Mum with us to the scan? That way it'll be just you and Christopher and Mum will get to see her grandchild. Not that she'll remember.' The husky note had crept back into Trish's voice.

'I'm so sorry, Trish. It's hard to watch, isn't it?'

'The worst,' Trish agreed. 'She was such a great grandmother, wasn't she? It's awful that my kids are never going to know that. They'll only know the shell she's going to become.'

Tess thought back to how wonderful the older woman had been with Ryan. How the two of them had been practically inseparable. How he'd hung on her every word and Jean had declared him the most loveable child on the planet.

No bias, of course.

'But you'll keep the real her alive for them, Trish.

You and Fletch. You'll tell them all about the wonder-ful, smart, kind, funny person she was and how very, very much she loves them. That person's always going to live inside you.'

'I know,' Trish murmured. 'Sorry. It just gets to me on some days more than others. I blame the hormones.'

Trish laughed and Tess joined in. It wasn't very jolly laughter but it broke the maudlin conversation.

'We'll be half an hour,' Tess said.

'Perfect.'

Tess hung up the phone and looked at Jean and the small pile of white sugar flowers on the bench top. 'Let's go and visit Trish,' she said.

'Oh, yes,' Jean said, her eyes sparkling. 'Yes, please.'

Tess was nervous as she and Jean walked up the stairs of Trish and Doug's massive, beautifully renovated Old Queenslander. Not even the warm welcome of the big, wide wraparound verandas helped to quell the low-level nausea that had afflicted her ever since she'd bundled Jean into the car.

But they were here now and then Trish was opening the front door and ushering them inside. She followed them down the hallway past rooms that Tess assumed to be bedrooms running off either side and into a large lounge with soaring ceilings. A dining room and kitchen spilled off the edges in a very open-plan arrangement.

'Wow. This is beautiful,' Tess commented as the warm honey of the polished floorboards and the rich tapestry of Middle-Eastern rugs attracted her attention.

Trish smiled. 'Thanks. It's been a labour of love.'

Tess remembered the cottage that she and Fletch had been renovating together and understood the pride and accomplishment on Trish's face.

'So, Christopher is asleep on the lounge. I've just given him something for the fever.' Trish half turned and indicated the little sleeping figure on the lounge chair behind her.

Tess looked over but kept her distance. Christopher was wearing just a nappy and lying on a sheet that had been tucked into the lounge cushions. A ceiling fan directly overhead blew a cool breeze downwards, ruffling white-blond hair with two little cowlicks.

Trish padded towards her son and gently stroked his forehead. She grimaced at the fine red rash sprinkling his torso. 'The doctor assures me the rash is a post-viral thing.'

Tess nodded absently. He looked so still. An image of Ryan in PICU popped into her head—so still and pale—and for a second Tess wasn't sure she could do it.

Then Trish turned to her and smiled. 'Thanks so much for doing this, Tess.' Her hand stroked her belly. 'It means so much to Doug and me.'

Tess smiled and assured her it was fine.

She handed Tess a piece of paper. 'Mobile numbers. Mine and Doug's. Just, you know…if you need to know where the pickles are or something.' She smiled at Tess then crossed into the kitchen. 'He can have a drink of water and a cup of milk if he wakes up and if he's hungry I've made up a couple of different things to tempt him in the fridge too—he's been off his food.'

Trish opened the fridge and indicated the stacked tower of plastic containers that looked like they could feed a small nation.

'Thanks. I'll try him if he wakes.'

Doug, who had entered the kitchen, rolled his eyes at Tess. 'Is she showing you the food she prepared for the masses?'

The knot of nervous tension eased slightly at Doug's teasing and Tess even laughed.

'We have to go, darling,' he reminded his wife, his arm slipping around Trish's non-existent waist.

Trish looked over at her son and Tess could tell that leaving him when he was sick was a real wrench for her. She remembered how that felt.

'Okay, let's go,' Trish murmured. 'Mum?'

Jean had found a little jug and was watering Trish's indoor plants. 'Yes, dear?'

'Let's go,' she said.

Jean smiled at her daughter. Then she frowned. 'Where are we going?'

'To the hospital. For the scan.' Trish patted her big round belly.

'Oh, yes,' Jean said. 'Splendid. We can drop Tess at work for her shift while we're at it.'

Tess smiled at Jean. 'I've got a day off today so I'm going to stay and look after Christopher.'

Jean looked down at her sleeping grandson. She frowned and looked up at Tess, perplexed. 'What a sweet boy,' she said vaguely.

Trish sighed. 'C'mon, Mum,' she murmured, laying a gentle hand beneath her mother's elbow and ushering her along. She smiled at Tess. 'See you in a couple of hours.'

Tess nodded, then the door closed behind them and then it was just her.

And Christopher.

Tess sat on the edge of the couch opposite Christopher. She felt awkward at first, desperately looking around the room at anything and everything other than him. Art on the walls. A DVD collection. Some bookshelves.

A set of open French doors led out onto a massive deck. Tess could see a tangle of wild, lush greenery from this vantage point and suddenly wished she was out there, digging in Trish's garden, not in here, looking after her most treasured possession.

But she daren't leave him. He looked so still and pale.

She sat back and pulled a book out of her handbag, determined to distract herself with Fletch's crime novel, which she still hadn't managed to finish.

Or would try to, at least.

But inevitably her gaze was drawn to the sleeping cherub. His little bow mouth, so like Ryan's, clutched at her heart. She dropped her gaze to focus on his chest, watching for the barely perceptible rise and fall, felt the hot spurt of panic as an occasional respiratory pause delayed the onset of the next breath.

Tess shook herself as she realised she was counting Christopher's breaths.

She returned her attention to the book with renewed vigour and for twenty minutes, apart from the odd sneak peek, she managed it. The story finally pulled her in and the only sounds breaking the silence were the fan whirring overhead, magpies warbling in the back yard and the rustle of paper as she turned a page.

Then Christopher stirred. Then he woke and sat up. He took one look at Tess and his bottom lip dropped, his forehead wrinkled.

'Mumma, Mumma,' he called, looking around wildly for Trish.

Tess's heart banged noisily against her ribs as she stood to comfort the child who, for all intents and purposes, was her nephew. 'It's okay, Christopher,' she crooned, approaching him slowly as he started to cry. 'Mummy and Daddy will be home very soon.'

She sat down beside him and he cried louder.

'I know, honey, I know. You're not feeling well, you just want your mummy.' She put her arm tentatively around his skinny little shoulders. They were warm beneath her cool palm. 'She'll be here really soon.'

Then Christopher really lost it. He screwed his face up, which went as red as the rash covering his body, and howled for all he was worth. Within seconds his eyes were streaming and his nose was running and he'd shrugged her hand away.

The poor little guy looked utterly miserable.

She suddenly understood Trish's earlier reticence as the crying child made her feel completely inadequate. Christopher didn't know her. So how could she console him properly? Mild panic set in at the thought that he might cry for the entire time Trish and Doug were away.

No. Think, Tess.

Think!

She'd been a paediatric nurse, for crying out loud. And a mother!

Yes. What would she have done if this had been Ryan? The problem was she'd fought so hard not to think about her son over the years it was as if all that basic maternal intuition had also been suppressed.

Come on, Tess, think!

Distraction.

Yes, distraction.

'Would you like a drink, sweetie?' she asked over the din.

Christopher showed no sign that he'd even heard the question so Tess hurried to the kitchen and retrieved the two plastic sippy cups from the fridge. She sat back down again and offered them to Christopher.

He pushed them both away. 'Are you sure?' Tess asked, offering them again.

Christopher looked at them, then at her, then back at them as his crying died down. He looked at her with red eyes and pointed to the milk. Tess smiled at him and handed it over. He took it on a shuddery indrawn breath and drank half the cup without pause.

'Good boy,' Tess murmured. 'More?'

Christopher went again, slower this time, his huge green eyes never leaving her face. When he'd finished he thrust the cup back at her.

'Are you hungry? Would you like something to eat?'

Christopher shook his head then pointed to the stack of books sitting on the nearby coffee table.

Tess smothered a smile. Christopher obviously knew what he wanted. Ryan had been like that too.

Fletch had called it stubborn. She'd called it decisive.

'You want me to read to you?' He nodded and she picked up the first book. 'This one?' she asked. He shook his head. He shook it four times before one met with his approval. 'You like cars?' she asked as she opened the book.

'Car, car,' Christopher said, nodding his head.

So Tess read it to him. On the first read-through he sat upright beside her, his little legs out in front of him, his ankles just dangling over the edge of the couch cushion. The next time he leaned in closer so his side was jammed against hers. By the third read he'd climbed into her lap.

Tess froze as he snuggled down, making himself at home. She hadn't held a child in a decade and it felt so bitter-sweet. Looking down on his blond head, she had a feeling of déjà vu, like holding Ryan all over again.

She pressed her nose to his hair, feeling the fine

down that stuck up at the crown tickle her nose as she inhaled deeply. The sweet little-boy smell lodged in her throat and when he turned his face up to look at her, unshed tears shone in her eyes.

'Car,' he prompted, one little pudgy finger pointing at the words.

Tess bit down on her lip. 'Car,' she murmured, swallowing hard against all the emotion and memories.

Eventually Christopher allowed her to read some other books but after about half an hour he started to feel very warm against her and started to grizzle. Tess felt his forehead.

'Gosh,' she murmured, 'you're burning up.'

She laid him on the lounge and reached for the tympanic thermometer that was also sitting on the coffee table. Christopher lay docilely as she inserted it into his ear canal and waited for it to beep. She read the display and was shocked to see his fever had spiked rapidly—no wonder he was lethargic and looking miserable again.

Trish had said she'd just given him something for the fever before she'd left so that was out as an option to bring the temperature down. Maybe a tepid sponge would help and also be soothing for Christopher.

'It's okay, sweetie. Tess is going to get you something nice and cool. Won't be a moment.'

Tess looked over her shoulder as she scurried towards the kitchen. Christopher lay quietly on the cushion, his gaze tracking her movements. In less than a minute she'd found a glass bowl in a cupboard and filled it with lukewarm water. Under the sink she'd located an unopened packet of dishcloths.

Christopher hadn't moved as she hurried towards him but he was staring now, his gaze not fixed any more. He looked out of it and an itch prickled at the bottom of her spine. She was two paces from him when he let out a little cry and his limbs stiffened.

Tess gasped and dropped the bowl, water spreading over the floorboards, soaking into the rug, as Christopher went into a full-blown seizure.

Tess lunged for the lounge. 'Christopher? Christopher!' she shouted as she threw herself down next to him.

His little body twitched and jerked and her brain came to a complete standstill as terror rendered her utterly useless.

'Christopher,' she whimpered again, not even game to touch him.

Oh, God, oh, God, oh, God!
Don't die, don't die, don't die.

She watched in horror, completely paralysed. She couldn't think what to do. She didn't know how to make him stop.

Some latent part of her brain was screaming at her and it finally made itself heard.

Ambulance.

Tess picked up her phone that she'd put on the coffee table earlier and with useless, trembling fingers somehow managed to dial three zeros. A voice she could barely hear over the roar of her pulse in her head asked her if she wanted police, fire or ambulance, and she knew she was yelling but she just couldn't stop. 'Ambulance, ambulance, ambulance.'

She tried not to think about another time, another call she'd made to triple zero. She'd been an incoherent mess then too.

Another voice came on seconds later. 'I need an ambulance now!' she told the voice frantically. 'My nephew is having a seizure.'

The soothing female voice asked her name and the address. For an awful moment Tess couldn't even remember the number of Trish's house—she just knew which one it was in the street as it had been so long since she'd needed to know. But in a blinding flash she remembered.

'Number sixteen,' she panted. 'Please, please, hurry, you must hurry. He's still fitting.'

The voice told her a car had already been dispatched with lights and sirens but it didn't reassure her. Tess looked down at Christopher, whose stiff, jerky movements continued unabated. How long had it been? Too long. It felt like for ever.

His lips lost their pinkness and Tess wailed into the phone, 'His lips are turning blue.'

'Okay, here's what I want you to do…'

Somehow Tess managed to follow the instructions from the emergency call-taker. Quite how, she wasn't sure. Her fingers were shaking, the roar in her head made it almost impossible to hear and she wanted to throw up. But putting Christopher on the floor and turning him on his side improved his colour even if it didn't stop the seizure.

All stuff that Tess knew but was too panicked to do herself.

'Why isn't it stopping?' she demanded of the woman who had assured Tess repeatedly that she would stay on the phone with her until the ambulance arrived. 'It should be stopped by now.'

As if speaking it had made it so, the jerking reduced to twitching and then stopped altogether. 'It's stopped,' Tess announced victoriously into the phone. 'It's stopped.'

'Okay, that's good,' the calm voice continued in her

ear. 'Keep him on his side. He'll be very sleepy for a while. The ambulance is about a minute out.'

Suddenly Tess heard a siren. 'I can hear it!' Her insides practically went to water at the relief that coursed through her system.

'Okay, I'm going to go now. Go and open the door for the paramedics.'

Tess nodded. 'Thank you,' she gasped. 'Thank you so much.' The connection had been momentary but in those awful minutes the stranger's voice had been a lifeline.

Tess pushed the 'end' button then hurried to the front door to greet the paramedics coming in through the front gate.

'This way,' she said. 'The seizure's just stopped.'

The paramedics greeted her as they crossed to a limp-looking Christopher lying on his side on the beautiful Turkish carpet that Tess had admired when she'd first arrived.

It seemed like an age ago now.

They knelt beside him, one in a puddle of water, and Tess apologised profusely. He smiled at her. 'It's okay, it'll dry,' he assured her.

They were hooking Christopher up to a monitor and trying to rouse him when he cried out again, his little limbs stiffening for the second time. 'He's going again,' the female paramedic said.

Tess clamped a hand over her mouth to muffle her wail as she looked on in abject terror. The paramedic kneeling in the water spoke into his radio. 'This is one five three. About to administer midazolam. ETA on the ICP.'

Tess couldn't watch. She just couldn't watch. She

needed…she needed Fletch. And, oh, God, she had to tell Trish!

How was she going to tell Trish?

Fletch would tell her. Fletch would know what to do.

She grabbed for her phone as the paramedics worked on Christopher. She turned her back, walked out to the front veranda. She couldn't look. She just couldn't. And he was in better hands with them than he had been with her.

She'd been utterly useless.

She dialled Fletch's number, her hands shaking so hard she had to try three times before she was successful. It went to voice mail. 'Fletch, it's Tess. You need to ring me urgently. Urgently!'

If she'd been in her right mind she wouldn't have left such an alarming message. Or the five more that followed. But she wasn't.

Another ambulance pulled up and a single paramedic raced into the house. Tess heard them say that Christopher had stopped breathing. That they were going to have to intubate.

A terrible foreboding settled over her. Déjà vu. Ryan all over again.

God! Where was Fletch?

She dialled his number again. 'Fletch! Damn it, ring me!'

She walked back in the house. Christopher had stopped seizing but they had a mask over his face and were puffing air into his lungs. The female paramedic was inserting an IV. The newcomer paramedic looked up at her standing by the door.

'He's stopped breathing. It's probably the drug we used to stop him fitting. It happens sometimes. We're going to put a tube into his lungs to help him breathe.'

Tess nodded. She knew all this, had seen it a hundred times. But this was Ryan.

No. No, wait. She blinked. *Christopher.* It was Christopher.

'Just hurry,' she urged, standing by the door her hands curled into fists. 'Hurry!'

Tess couldn't look away now. She sank to the floor and watched while they put a tube down Christopher's throat, exactly like they'd done with Ryan. Her heart was banging so loudly her whole body seemed to bob to its rhythm. She could hear the blip, blip, blip of Christopher's heart rate on the monitor and almost collapsed on the floor when the intensive care paramedic announced, 'I'm in. Let's get this tube secured so we can scoop and go.'

In five minutes they had Christopher on a trolley and were heading out the door. 'We're taking him to St Rita's. Do you want to come with us in the ambulance?' the female paramedic asked.

Tess wanted to shake her head. Christopher was in safe hands and she wanted to run away. Go straight to the airport and get a ticket back to the UK. Her head felt like it was about to explode. Her heart was being ripped to shreds in her chest.

But she couldn't leave him. He looked small and pale and fragile dwarfed by all the medical equipment and she couldn't leave him alone. She nodded and followed them in a daze. She didn't take her bag or even shut the front door.

Tess sat in the front seat as the ambulance sped away from the kerb, lights and siren on. The intensive care paramedic and the female paramedic—they'd told her their names but she couldn't remember them—were in the back, tending to Christopher.

Her phone rang and the sudden noise was so star-tling she stared at it for a moment, trying to remember what it was. Fletch's name was flashing on the screen as Tess looked at it and suddenly she realised what she was holding and relief washed through her like a rag-ing tsunami. She pushed the answer button in a rush.

'Fletch?'

'What's wrong?' he asked, his voice frantic after eight missed calls from Tess with increasingly alarm-ing messages. 'Is it Mum?'

It took a moment for Tess to figure out why Fletch would think something was up with Jean. But, of course, he hadn't known of her plans to look after his nephew. 'No. It's Christopher.'

'Christopher?'

'It's a long story,' she said, suddenly so strung out from an excess of adrenaline she just wanted to curl up in a foetal position somewhere and rock.

'Is that a siren?' Fletch demanded.

Tess ignored him. 'I've been looking after him for a couple of hours while Trish went for her scan. He had a…a convulsion. They gave him midaz… He stopped breathing. They… they t-tubed him, Fletch. We're in an ambulance on our way to St Rita's.'

She swallowed hard as a lump of emotion bigger than the iceberg that sank the Titanic lodged in her throat. 'I'm scared, Fletch.'

Fletch gripped the phone, trying to assimilate what Tess was telling him. She sounded close to hysteria and he shut his eyes, knowing that whatever had happened today Tess wasn't emotionally equipped to deal with it.

'It's going to be okay, Tess,' he assured her, even though he had absolutely no idea what the hell was going on. 'I'm coming downstairs,' he said, already abandoning the computer work he'd been doing and striding out of the unit. 'I'll be waiting for you when you pull in.'

Tess could feel the tight control she'd been keeping in place slowly unravel as Fletch's calm, soothing voice spoke assurances into her ear.

'Promise?' she demanded. 'Promise you'll be there?'

'I promise.' He paused for a moment. 'Are you okay, Tess?'

Tess shook her head. She was about as far from okay as was physically possible. 'No. But as long as you're there, I will be.' She was surprised to realise just how true that was.

'I'll be there.'

Tess had never heard three more beautiful words in her life.

CHAPTER NINE

FLETCH drummed his fingers impatiently against his thigh as he stood in the ambulance bay, listening to the urgent wail of a siren draw closer and closer.

It couldn't get here soon enough.

His gut churned as worry about Tess's state of mind warred with his fear for Christopher.

What exactly had happened?

He'd left for work a few hours ago and Tess and Jean had been planning on doing some baking, and now he was standing outside the emergency department, waiting for his intubated nephew to arrive in the back of an ambulance with a frantic Tess in tow.

He should have known things had been going too well lately. His mother was content, the study was running smoothly and things with he and Tess were finally…easy.

It was a subtle difference, probably not noticeable to anyone else especially as, from the outside, he doubted anyone would have even noticed that things *hadn't been* easy.

It was just a feeling between them.

Ever since she'd comforted him that night, things had changed between them. The awkwardness that had been there since she'd come back to live with him, which had been exacerbated by the kiss and which they'd ploughed through every day to keep things as normal as possible for Jean, had dissipated.

In all the small ways it felt just like they were married again. Finding mango ice cream in the freezer, putting toothpaste on her toothbrush when he brushed his teeth just like he used to do, a shared memory making them smile.

Even going to bed at night, which had been fraught with anxiety for him, had changed. He didn't wait now for her to be asleep before he came in or get up before she woke. They just got into bed together and went to sleep. Sometimes they talked a bit about their day or discussed Jean, other times they read companionably or she read while he worked on his laptop, but the apprehension was gone.

Or at least it had been.

The siren almost upon him, a portent of doom if ever he'd heard one, was a sign that the dynamic had shifted again. And whatever ground they'd gained was about to be lost.

Maybe for ever.

The siren was killed as the ambulance screamed into the bay. A paramedic jumped from the vehicle and hurried to the back doors, a doctor and a nurse from Emergency joining him there. Fletch headed straight for the front passenger door and opened it. A pale-faced Tess looked down at him with a dazed expression.

'Tess!'

Relief stormed his system. He'd been half-crazy, listening to those increasingly desperate messages. He'd expected her to be a hysterical mess, like she'd been that day with Ryan. Seeing her dry-eyed and relatively calm was a miracle.

It shouldn't be—this was classic Tess after all. Stoic. Controlled. Keeping it all together.

But what she'd just been through would have shaken anyone. Especially someone who'd already been through something this terrible before.

'Are you okay?' he asked as he held out his hand to help her down.

'I don't know what happened,' she said, shaking her head at him as her feet touched the ground. 'He just started fitting.'

Her frightened, confused face grabbed at his gut and an overwhelming urge to protect her coursed through him. He swept her into arms and kissed the top of her head. 'It's fine. He's going to be fine.'

Tess sagged against him, absorbing the heat and the solidity of him. Remembering how good it always felt, how right. 'I didn't know what I was supposed to do, Fletch. I was useless.'

Fletch pulled away slightly, grasping her upper arms, and put his face close to hers so he could make sure she understood what he was about to say. 'You called the ambulance, didn't you?' She nodded, and he acknowledged it with a brisk nod of his own. 'That's what you were supposed to do.'

Tess bit her lip. *She would not cry.* She wouldn't.

'I was so scared it was like…it was like Ryan. All I could see was Ryan lying there. Ryan's blond hair. Ryan's blue lips.'

Fletch pulled her in close again as those images, never far away, rolled through his mind. He'd give anything at this moment to have erased what she'd just been through. No one should have to go through something so shocking twice.

'I'm sorry you had to go through that, Tess. I'm so

sorry. But you did good. Trish couldn't have left Ryan in safer hands.'

Tess pulled away from him on a gasp. 'Oh, God, Fletch. Trish! I haven't… I couldn't call her. She doesn't know yet.'

Fletch nodded, already dreading that conversation. 'It's okay, I'll call her. Let's go inside and find out what's happening then I'll call her, okay?'

'Okay.'

She followed him in on autopilot. Into the resus bay where staff swarmed around Christopher, loading him with anti-epileptic drugs and putting in another IV. It looked like chaos but Tess knew that everyone there had a job and that their teamwork would get Christopher through.

Still, she found it hard to breathe. Resus looked the same as it had ten years ago when they'd brought Ryan here, and she couldn't stand it. Flashbacks flared in her head as a doctor fired questions at her just like they had with Ryan.

Yes, a virus. No, she didn't know how long he'd been unwell for. No, she didn't know if he'd ever had a febrile convulsion before. Fletch thought not. Yes, his temp had spiked. No, she didn't know how long he'd had the rash for or how many wet nappies he'd had that day.

They went on and on until there was a roaring so loud in her ears she could barely hear them. She turned to Fletch, who was talking to a colleague, and tugged on his sleeve. 'I can't stay here,' she said. 'I can't…do this. Get me…get me out of here.'

Fletch saw the shadows in her eyes and the tautness around her mouth. 'Come on,' he said, putting his arm around her.

He led her outside. 'Margie, can I use your office?'

he asked a middle-aged matronly woman in a nurse's uniform striding by.

Margie narrowed her eyes for a moment but Tess could only assume she must have looked close to a nervous breakdown because the woman didn't hesitate. 'First on the left at the end of the corridor,' she said briskly.

Fletch made a beeline for the office and had Tess ensconced in a chair in twenty seconds flat. He crouched in front of her. 'The consultant thinks it's just fever related and that Christopher decided not to breathe properly after the midaz dose. They're going to wait for him to wake up and then pull the tube.' He placed a hand on her knee and gave it a squeeze. 'He's going to be fine, Tess.'

She nodded. She'd heard the consultant telling Fletch as much. It was just taking a little while to work through the soup that her brain had become.

Fletch frowned. He'd thought she'd be over the moon at the news. 'Tess?'

'Yes.' She nodded. 'I know. That's great.' She smiled at him. 'Really great. It's just a lot to…absorb, you know?'

Yes, he did know. And she was in shock, which probably made it that much harder. 'I'm going to call Trish. Will you be all right in here?'

Tess nodded vigorously. 'Of course. Go, call your sister.' She consulted her watch. 'They must be on their way home by now.'

He was back in ten minutes and Tess looked at him expectantly. 'How is she?'

He shoved his fingers through his hair. 'Pretty frantic. They've just got out of the scan. They're coming straight here. They're only five minutes away.'

Five minutes but Tess knew it would feel like an age to Trish. She knew intimately how her sister-in-law would be feeling. The lead in her belly, the tightness in her chest, the rampant fear knotting every muscle.

The if-onlys.

If only I'd been there. If only I'd cancelled the scan today. If only I'd taken him to the hospital for a second opinion.

Fletch sat beside her and Tess looked at him. 'What are you doing?' she asked.

'I'll wait with you until they get here,' he said.

Tess shook her head. 'No.' She pushed his arm, urging him to get up. 'You can't leave him in there by himself, Fletch.'

'He's surrounded by people, Tess.'

Fletch knew his nephew was in good hands but he didn't have a clue what was going on in Tess's head. He could do nothing for Christopher now—he was being taken care of by experts.

But he could be here for Tess.

She shook her head vigorously. 'Not by people who love him. He's so small, Fletch. He looks so tiny and fragile surrounded by all that...stuff.' She pushed at his arm again. 'You have to be there with him. Don't let him be alone.'

Fletch didn't dare argue. She was breathing hard and there were two bright red spots high on her spare cheekbones. She hadn't wanted to leave Ryan alone either. Not even after he'd been declared dead. She'd sat for ages and just held his hand.

'Okay, Tess,' he said quietly as he stood. 'It's okay, I will. I'll be with him until Trish arrives. Apparently they have Mum...' In all the drama Fletch had temporarily forgotten about his mother. 'So I'll bring her back here to be with you if you don't mind?'

Tess nodded. 'Of course. Just go,' she urged again.

Tess checked her watch every minute for the next fifteen as the four walls pushed in on her. She read the posters for hand washing and a couple of anti-violence ones designed to warn emergency department patients that violence against staff would not be tolerated.

A wall-mounted bookshelf was crammed with thick, heavy textbooks. Some had fallen over and others were leaning drunkenly against each other. The desk was controlled chaos with a lot of paper and a computer displaying a screensaver.

A cork board behind the door had postcards and work photos tacked to it. Smiling nurses and doctors snapped in the middle of their jobs or temporarily acting the fool for the lens.

It looked like a happy work place. Where people liked each other and got along.

But how anybody could deal with the kind of things that came through those doors, things like Christopher—and Ryan—and stay as normal as the snaps suggested was beyond Tess.

They all deserved medals.

Or to have their heads read.

Fletch appeared in the doorway with a worried-looking Jean and a red-eyed Trish. 'Here's Tess,' he said to his mother, injecting a light note into his tone.

'Oh, Tess, there you are.' Jean's voice was light with relief. 'I don't know why we're at the hospital, do you?'

Tess smiled reassuringly at her then looked over Fletch's shoulder to a devastated Trish. She looked like she was close to collapse and it was only Fletch's arm around her waist that was holding her up.

'It's okay, Jean,' Tess said, focusing back on her mother-in-law. 'I'm going to take you home. I think Tabby needs to be walked.'

'Oh, goodness, yes!'

'Just have a seat here for a sec,' Tess said, helping Jean into the chair, 'And we'll be on our way in a jiffy.'

Jean sat down with minimum fuss, which left Tess facing Trish. It was like looking in a mirror. 'How's he doing?' she asked.

'Oh, Tess,' Trish wailed, her face crumpling as she pulled Tess into her arms and gave her a fierce squeeze. 'He looks so small.'

Tess stared over Trish's shoulder at Fletch as his sister purged her emotions. 'I'm sorry,' Tess murmured, hugging her tight. 'I'm so sorry.'

'No,' Trish said, pulling back and wiping at her tears with the backs of her hands. 'This is not your fault, Tess. It was a febrile convulsion. I need to thank you. Thank you for being there. I would have been completely useless.'

Tess shook her head. 'I just called the ambulance.'

Trish nodded. 'Exactly.' She pulled a tissue out of her pocket and blew her nose. 'I know this can't have been easy for you today, Tess. Looking after Christopher was a huge step for you and then to have this happen… it must have bought up a lot of stuff with Ryan that I know you don't like to think about.'

Tess froze at the mention of her son. She'd been trying so hard not to think of him during this whole ordeal but the very essence of him was building inside her, demanding to be let out, and she just couldn't let it.

'It's fine,' she dismissed quickly.

She didn't want to get into this. Not now. Not ever.

Trish shook her head. 'I don't think I could survive if something happened to Christopher. I don't know how you've managed, Tess.'

Tess looked over Trish's shoulder at a grim-looking Fletch. 'Some would say I haven't managed very well at all.'

'Then they don't know what it's like, do they?'

Tess glanced back at her sister-in-law. 'No, they don't.'

Trish sniffled and wiped her nose with the tissue again. 'I have to go…I have to get back to Christopher. Doug's not very good in hospitals. They're transferring Christopher to the PICU where they're hoping they'll be able to take the tube out in a couple of hours.'

Tess nodded. 'Best place for him. Give him a kiss for me.'

'Do you want to… Do you want to come and see him?'

Tess recoiled from the suggestion. Circumstances had dictated that she be part of this nightmare scenario but now it was over, she just wanted to put it away in the same place she put her Ryan stuff.

Deep down and out of reach.

Besides, Jean was getting restless, pacing around the small office and anxiously asking every ten seconds when they could leave.

'Ah, no. I'm going to get Jean home. I think the stress of this environment is increasing her anxiety level and you guys just need to be able to think about Christopher today.'

Trish nodded. 'Take our car,' she said as she reached into her handbag for her set of keys. 'It's parked in the

two-minute emergency parking and needs shifting anyway, and it's not like we're going anywhere soon.'

'Thanks,' Tess said, taking the keys.

'I'll follow shortly,' Fletch said.

Tess shook her head. 'No, Fletch, you need to stay
with Trish—she needs you now. So does Doug.'

It was such a cowardly thing to set him up for. She
couldn't bear to do it herself so she was putting it on him
when she knew it had to be just as difficult for Fletch
to go into the PICU—as a relative, not a doctor—and
sit with his sister while she watched a machine breathe
for her little boy.

A little boy that looked remarkably like his own little boy.

It was cowardly to ask him to have to relive the whole
nightmare of Ryan again while she fled to the safety
of home.

But Trish and Doug shouldn't go through it by themselves either, not when they had someone with a wealth
of ICU experience in the family. Not when they'd been
such a tower of strength to her and Fletch a decade before.

Trish needed her brother now.

And, yes, she probably needed Tess now too, but
Tess had given all she could.

'I'd like you to stay, Fletch,' Trish whispered. 'I'm
sorry, I know that's asking a lot.'

Fletch smiled at his sister. 'Of course.' He squeezed
her shoulder. 'Whatever you need.'

'Are we going yet?' Jean asked again.

Tess nodded briskly. 'Yes, we're going right now.
Come on, let's be off.'

She gave Trish a quick hug, mouthed 'Thank you'

to Fletch and then ushered Jean out the door and didn't look back.

'I'm sorry, Fletch,' Trish said as they watched the two women disappear around the corner. 'Will she be okay?'

Fletch grimaced. 'I don't know, Trish. I don't know how much longer she can go on like this, just keeping it all bottled up, keeping it all inside.'

Trish squeezed his hand. 'You still love her, don't you?'

He looked down at his little sister as her words seemed to make sense of the jumble of emotions that had been tangoing inside him since Tess had been back in his life. 'I don't think I ever stopped.'

And the guilt he felt at what he had done all those years ago magnified tenfold.

Tess kept busy when she got back to the apartment.

Busy, busy, busy.

They walked Tabby, baked a double batch of muffins—one for Trish and Doug—and then cooked a huge lasagne for tea, half of which could also go to Trish. They cleaned up the kitchen and watched Jean's television game shows. They took Tabby down again for one last toilet stop before bedtime.

Normally Tess loved the river at this hour of the late afternoon as the shadows turned it an inky velvet and she and Jean and Fletch too, if he was home, would watch it for a long time, chatting about the different boats, and Jean would usually tell a story from her childhood.

But Tess didn't want to indulge in anything that didn't involve brisk activity. The events of the day had stirred up too many memories and if she stood still for too long they might just take over.

When they returned to the apartment Fletch still wasn't home. Tess felt a spike of worry and pushed it away.

It would be fine. Christopher would be fine.

They ate the lasagne without him, Jean doing him up a plate and covering it with cling film just as she always used to when she'd come to stay with them and he was on shift. Then she washed up.

'Oh look, *Vertigo* is on,' Jean said, pointing to the television as she dried her hands on a tea towel. 'Jimmy Stewart is magnificent in it, don't you think?'

Tess marvelled over the complexities of the human memory and the bizarre progression of a disease like Alzheimer's. Earlier Jean hadn't known what a whisk was but she could remember a film that was over fifty years old.

'Shall we watch it?' Tess asked.

Fletch still hadn't returned by the time the movie faded to black and Jean declared she was off to bed. Tess watched as she and Tabby headed for the bedroom.

Then there was just her, a quiet apartment and the relentless pulse inside her of things she didn't want to think about.

She texted Fletch. *Everything okay?*

He texted back. *Extubated twenty minutes ago. Will be home soon.*

Tess didn't know if she was relieved that he would be coming home soon or not. It was good to know that Christopher had been successfully extubated but it had been a momentous day and she was pretty sure Fletch was going to be physically and mentally exhausted.

She remembered how shattered he'd been that night after being woken to do the study consent on the immersion. How much worse would he be after hours in the very PICU where his son had died, watching as a machine pumped air into a carbon copy of him?

She took a shower and tried not to think about it. She hummed out loud to keep the images of Christopher and Ryan at bay as they rose and blurred in her head unbidden. She scrubbed at her body vigorously with the towel afterwards, rubbed at her hair so hard the sound of it temporarily obliterated everything else from her head.

Then she heard 'Tess?' and her heart contracted with the force of a sonic boom then tripped along at a crazy clip.

Fletch.

'In here,' she called out. 'Just a sec.'

She looked around the bathroom for something to wear. With Fletch not home yet, she hadn't thought to bring her pyjamas in with her. There were two options—the towel she was using or the T-shirt he'd been wearing to bed, which he'd hung on the towel rack that morning and had left there.

She shied away from the whole idea of the towel. A towel said *I'm naked under here.* A T-shirt said *I'm dressed.*

So she quickly threw it over her head and was immediately surrounded by the very essence of Fletch. That strange mix of aftershave and deodorant and pheromones that all combined to make a wild, heady aroma. She inhaled deeply and her nipples tightened against the fabric, rubbing erotically on the inside where his own naked skin had imprinted.

Dear God! Get a grip.

She'd worn his shirts a hundred times in the past and with what they'd been through today her nipples and his pheromones shouldn't even be registering.

She was just stalling.

And she doubted he'd even notice.

'Hi,' she said as she stepped out of the bathroom, flicking the light out and leaving just her bedside lamp to illuminate the room. He was sitting on his side of the bed, taking his shoes off, his back to her.

'Hi,' he said, turning to look at her. She was in his shirt and a rush of emotion filled his chest. He wanted to lose himself in her so badly at the moment he had to turn away from her lest she see it and run screaming out of the apartment.

'You're wearing my shirt,' he said, for something to say other than *I love you.*

Tess grimaced. *So much for him not noticing.* 'Yes. Sorry. It was…at hand.'

'Don't apologise,' he said. 'My shirts always looked better on you.'

Tess walked around the bed, approaching his side tentatively. She stopped when she was standing in front of him an arm's length away. 'Are you okay?' she asked his downcast head.

He lifted his head and pierced her with his wattle-green eyes. 'What do you think?' he demanded, his voice low.

Tess looked at him. His salt-and-pepper three-day growth looked more salt suddenly, his eyes bloodshot and the lines on his forehead and around his mouth deeper. His tie was pulled askew, his top button undone and it looked like he'd worn a track in his hair from constant finger ploughing.

'I'm sorry,' she whispered. 'I just couldn't…I couldn't stay.'

Fletch reached out a hand and squeezed her forearm, dropping it again straight away. 'I know. You did enough today…it's fine.'

'Is he okay?'

Fletch nodded. 'Grizzly but curled up in Trish's lap in a recliner by the bed when I left.'

Tess visibly sagged at the news—she hadn't realised she'd been holding herself so upright. She knew from her past PICU experience that it would happen that way but the whole drama had been too close to home and deep down she'd been preparing herself for disaster.

'Oh...thank God,' she murmured, clutching a hand to her breast.

Fletch rubbed a hand through his hair and then scratched at his chin. It rasped like sandpaper in the still of the night. 'He's just so much like...Ryan, you know?' he said, marvelling at how Tess had managed to keep it together at Trish's today when it must have been the most horrendous experience for her.

'I just kept seeing him...Ryan. Looking at Christopher's chest rise and fall and thinking it was Ryan.'

Tess saw the moisture in his eyes and felt a corresponding moisture in hers. The tears she'd been trying to keep at bay all day—no, all decade—burned for release. But still she wouldn't let them. She'd already shed more than her allotted amount since coming to stay with Fletch.

And the tears threatening were world-is-nigh tears and she knew once she'd shed them there was no way back. That part of Ryan would go with them and as much as she tried not to think about him, she wanted to know he'd be there if and when she was ready.

'It was awful,' he murmured.

'I know,' she said, remembering how hard it had been to separate Ryan and Christopher in her own head. 'I know.'

And it seemed like the most natural thing in the world to take a step closer. To step right into the circle of his arms and enfold him in hers.

Fletch shut his eyes as she fitted against him. She cradled his head against the soft part where neck met shoulder, and he inhaled the scent of her. Her shampoo and her perfume and the strange heady mix of his shirt on her skin. He drew her close and just absorbed her.

He felt the kiss at his temple first. It was so light he didn't even realise for a moment. But his mouth must have because his lips were nuzzling her neck and then her fingers were in his hair and his hand was sliding down her back and she moaned in his ear as his hand skimmed her bare skin where buttock met thigh.

He pulled back, one hand clamped on the back of her leg, the other firmly on her opposite hip. His heart banged against his ribs as desire ran thick and undiluted to every nerve in his body.

'Tess?'

Tess read his question loud and clear and knew the answer even before he'd asked it. She could already feel the taint of the day sliding away with her inhibitions. The memories of Christopher and Ryan and ambulances and hospitals fading with every fan of his breath on her neck.

She couldn't remember a time when she'd needed him more.

CHAPTER TEN

'Make love to me,' she whispered.

Fletch drew in a shuddery breath at her request. That he could do—loving her had always been easy.

Loving her had never gone away.

He tilted his head, his gaze zeroing in on her mouth. The flesh of her thigh was hot and pliant beneath his palm and he squeezed. A tiny, almost imperceptible gurgle at the back of her throat went straight to his groin and his breath stuttered out between them.

He opened his palm and traced the inside of her thigh with his fingertips. He watched as she shivered and her eyes widened before fluttering closed. His fingers traced higher, over the sweet curve of a naked buttock, into the dip that formed the small of her back, across to the bony prominence of her hip.

Tess sucked in a breath. 'Fletch,' she murmured, opening her eyes.

Their gazes meshed as his fingers trailed upwards. The curve of her waist, the bumps of her spine, the fan of her ribs. Each slow, lazy stroke ruching his shirt ever northward.

Tess bit her lip as cool air caressed bare, heated flesh from her waist down. It pricked at her skin, leaving thousands of goose-bumps and two erect nipples in its wake.

'Lift your arms,' he whispered against her mouth.

She clutched his shoulder at his husky command. Long-forgotten muscles clenched deep inside. Then she did his bidding, slowly raising her arms above her head, her gaze never leaving his.

Fletch swallowed at the directness in her gaze and her complete compliance with his command. His palms skimmed up her sides, hooking his T-shirt as they went, past the swell of her breasts, up over her shoulders and finally over her head.

His breath hissed out as she stood between his legs totally naked.

He dropped his gaze to look at her. She was different now. Thinner, less round, her breasts smaller, her bones more prominent. But there was still a slight curve to her hips and her waist still dipped and her breasts were still dominated by large areolas that had deepened to mocha during her pregnancy and were as fascinating tonight as they'd always been. He swallowed, just anticipating taking them into his mouth.

He dropped a kiss at the hollow at the base of her throat and whispered, 'Tess,' against her neck, his erection straining painfully against the confines of his trousers. 'My Tess.'

Tess shut her eyes as his lips moved along a collar bone and his palms stroked up and down her back, urging her closer.

She *was* his Tess. Had *always* been his Tess.

He turned his head and made for the other collar bone and she whimpered as his hot tongue lapped at her skin like she was dusted with honey. Fletch pulled back, already breathing too hard as the aroma of her swirled around him in an intoxicating haze.

A trail of glistening skin shone in the lamplight

where he'd laved her collar bones but her mouth, so
tantalisingly close, looked parched in comparison. He
claimed it then, biting back on a groan as she instantly
granted him the entry he craved. His tongue plunged
inside then flicked over her lips, desperate to also make
them moist with his possession.

His hands slid down to her smooth bare bottom, pulling her pelvis into the cradle of his. One hand moved
lower, stroking down the backs of her thighs, the other
moved higher, seeking the fulfilment only a round female breast could offer.

Years ago one of her breasts would have spilled out
of his palm but now it fit perfectly, the hard nub in the
middle scraping erotically against the dead centre. He
squeezed it and she whimpered. He flicked his thumb
over the tightly ruched nipple and she cried out, breaking their lip lock.

'Fletch,' she moaned.

Fletch felt her fingers plough into his hair as he
kissed down her neck, homing in on his target. His
mouth salivated at the feast that awaited. His hand at the
back of her thigh moved up swiftly to her other breast
and by the time his mouth had closed over her nipple
his fingers had claimed the other.

Tess gasped, her knees buckling slightly. She felt his
arm tighten around her waist as she clasped his head
to her chest. Partly to stay upright, partly because she
did not want him to stop. The heat and the pull of his
mouth as he paid homage to her breasts was turning
everything liquid.

Her head spun as he continued to use his mouth and
tongue on nipples so aroused she wanted to throw her
head back and howl her pleasure. She dropped a hand
to his shoulder to steady herself, her palm instantly la-

menting the feel of thick starched fabric instead of hot male skin.

She opened her eyes, suddenly aware that whilst she was buck naked, he was still fully clothed.

That wouldn't do. It wouldn't do at all.

She groped for his buttons, her eyes rolling back as he switched attention from one nipple to the other, taking it from cool and puckered to hot and hard in a second as he sucked it deep into his throat.

Her fingers fumbled and somehow found his loosened tie despite the havoc he was creating. She only just managed to strip it out from his collar as his teeth grazed the sensitive tip in his mouth and she lost all coherent thought for a beat or two.

Determined to plough on whatever the provocation, Tess straddled his lap and started in on his buttons, pleased to hear a guttural groan escape his mouth as she rocked herself into him. He released the nipple he was torturing, placing his forehead against her chest and breathing hard as he grabbed her hips and held here there.

She smiled then slowly pushed at his shoulders until he was lying back on the mattress and she had him at her total mercy. His eyes, smoky with desire, glittered up at her as she rotated her pelvis again and he swore under his breath, his fingers gripping her hips hard.

She marvelled that ten years of abstinence hadn't dulled her sexual instincts. But, then, it had always been instinctive with Fletch. There'd been guys before him but they'd always been such hard work. With Fletch it had been easy.

So very, very easy.

Still, she'd have thought she'd be nervous about having sex again after such a long dry stretch. Or that she might even have forgotten how. But towering over Fletch's reclined form, she knew that her body knew what to do.

And she knew it was going to be better than ever.

Tess leaned forward slightly, her gaze locking with his as she reached for his first button. It popped easily and she lowered her mouth to where it had been and pressed a kiss there. She repeated the process with each button until they were all undone and his shirt had fallen open.

Fletch let out his breath on a hiss as she sat up to admire her handiwork and her breasts bobbed enticingly. Once upon a time her long hair would have flowed down her front and covered them and he liked it that they were free to his gaze. He reached up and traced a finger from her collar bone to the tip of a rapidly hardening nipple and repeated it on the other side.

She arched her back and thrust her hips forward a little, and he curled up to claim her mouth because he doubted she had a clue how provocative she looked, straddling him stark naked, her breasts thrust out, while he was practically still fully clothed. She whimpered against his mouth, opening to the insistent thrust of his tongue and the bruising crush of his lips as he ground his pelvis into hers.

Tess could barely breathe as the onslaught of Fletch's out-of-control kiss sucked away all her oxygen. She desperately dragged in air through her nostrils as she rode the wild bucking of his hips.

'Tess,' he groaned against her mouth.

Tess could feel the hard length of him rubbing against the centre of her splayed thighs and she wanted more. She wanted him naked and inside her. She didn't want the barrier of two layers of fabric and a metal zipper.

She wanted him thick and hard and proud the way she remembered him in dreams she couldn't always quell. She wanted to feel him in her hand. She wanted to relish every inch of him as he entered her and took her to a place far, far away from this world where they just didn't do things like this.

She broke away from his mouth, pushing him back again, more urgently this time. She looked down at his erection clearly outlined beneath the taut pull of fabric. She reached for it, walked her fingers up it, walked them back down.

'Tess.'

The growl was deep and low, stroking deep and low inside her as he looked at her from beneath half-shuttered eyelids.

She heeded his warning, quickly unbuckling his belt, popping the button and peeling back his zip. The opening of metal teeth was loud in a room where the only other noise was the rasp of breath.

One glimpse of the long hard length of him and she was pushing aside the flaps of his fly and grasping him still encased in his underwear. Her insides clenched and she rocked against him, a completely involuntary movement.

Fletch shut his eyes on a groan as she rubbed herself against his thigh while she stroked his thickness and then impatiently broke through the last barrier to put her hand around him, skin on skin. He cried out as the muscles in his groin and belly and deep inside his buttocks shuddered.

He vaulted up again, his hands sliding to her breasts, his mouth slamming into hers, their tongues thrusting as their hips rocked to a rhythm pounding simultaneously through both of their bloodstreams and she milked the length of him.

Fletch couldn't bear it a moment longer. It had been so long and he'd dreamed of them coming together again too many lonely nights to count. He grasped her thighs and tumbled her to the side, rolling on top of her in one easy movement.

'I need you,' he muttered against her neck.

'I'm yours,' she whispered straight into his ear.

Fletch felt everything stutter to a halt. He shut his eyes as the familiarity of the words slugged him right between the eyes. He felt her mouth at his neck and her hand pushing beneath the loosened waistband of his trousers, sliding beneath his jocks to grasp his buttocks, but everything inside him had turned cold.

The words played in his head over and over. A different place. A different time.

A different woman.

He saying, *I need you.* She saying, *I'm yours.*

It was like a blast of arctic air in his face. *He couldn't do it.* He couldn't go ahead with it. Because he knew with a certainty that came from deep in his bones that he loved Tess and he wanted more than this, more than one night.

He wanted every night.

He wanted his wife back.

But there were things that had to be said first.

It took a moment or two for Tess to realise that Fletch wasn't responding when she pressed her mouth to his. She pulled back. 'Fletch?'

Fletch looked down at her, a frown knitting her brows together. 'I'm sorry...' He dropped his head on her chest, giving himself a moment to take stock. 'I can't do this...' he said.

His voice was muffled but Tess could sense his with-drawal in every muscle of his body.

No, no, no. She mewed her disappointment as Fletch pushed himself away from her. *She needed this, damn it!*

Fletch's hands trembled as he gripped the side of the mattress, keeping his back to her. He tucked himself away with difficulty, pulling up the zip over his bulge, feeling instantly uncomfortable. His fingers shook as he did up a couple of buttons to cover his chest. He bent down and retrieved her shirt, *his shirt*, from the floor, dropping it behind him without looking.

The shirt landed on her belly, cold against her heated flesh, and Tess just stared at it for a moment. Her blood was still thrumming thick and sludgy through every cell in her body, rendering her completely useless.

'There's something you need to know,' he said, star-ing out at the darkness beyond his floor-to-ceiling win-dows.

Tess blinked at his back as a sense of foreboding pushed the sticky remnants of desire violently aside. She scrambled upright, throwing the shirt over her head, then wriggled off the bed to stand in front of him. 'Whatever it is, I don't want to know,' she said.

Because it didn't take a genius to figure out this was something to do with Ryan. She didn't want to talk about Ryan. Surely he knew that by now? She didn't want to think about him or reminisce about him. She didn't even want to say his name.

Didn't he realise how much it hurt to even say his name?

Fletch almost gave up. But that was what he'd al-ways done with her because her grief and her guilt had been so great he'd tried to make everything else easy for her. He'd let her avoid and deny and shut things out because she'd asked him to and he'd been at a loss as to how to help her.

Well, not any more.

He wanted something real with her. Warts and all. It meant making some hard decisions but he was finally going to fight for her instead of letting her slip away again. 'I need to talk about this.'

Tess crossed her arms. 'Damn it, Fletch, why do you think we're on your bed, making out like teenagers? Especially after today? So we don't have to talk.'

He shook his head. 'I don't believe you, Tess. You want more than that.'

'No,' she denied.

Fletch felt a wellspring of frustration and anger bubble up inside him at her stonewalling. 'Well, if all you wanted was for me to *screw* you then why did you ask me to make love to you?'

Tess blinked at his profanity. 'I guess because asking you to *screw* me was just a little too crass,' she hissed.

'Well, at least I would have known where I stood,' he snapped.

'Oh, come on, Fletch. You can't tell me you weren't trying to forget about today just a little bit too.'

Fletch snorted. He stood and stalked passed her, stopping in front of the windows, his reflection staring grimly back at him. *God, he looked like hell.*

He turned his back on it. 'I was doing what you asked me to do, Tess. I was *making love* to you.'

They stared at each other for long moments, their chests rising and falling rapidly, this time in anger.

Fletch ran a hand through his hair. 'It's not about Ryan,' he said. 'Not directly anyway.'

Because they both knew that everything in their lives since Ryan had always stemmed from Ryan.

'Don't, Fletch. Please, don't.'

He heard the plea in her voice and knew it would be so easy not to tell her. To take the coward's way out. He'd decided nine years ago to keep it to himself—why not just stick to it?

Because their relationship nine years ago had been a train wreck and he couldn't go there again.

He wanted to be with her, he wanted to make love to her.

But he couldn't make love to her with this on his conscience.

It's why he'd walked away all those years ago without a fight.

They had a lot of work to do with their relationship. A lot of honesty and dealing with their unresolved grief and unspoken feelings around Ryan. There was going to be a lot of soul-searching and it demanded total honesty.

And that had to start now.

Fletch knew it was the only way they could build a relationship that could survive and thrive the second time around. And if he had to drag her kicking and screaming along with him, he would.

Because he knew deep down that she still loved him too.

And this time he was fighting for that love.

'I'll give you fair warning. I'm not just going to let you disappear out of my life again, Tess.'

Tess blinked at his audacity. 'You don't get a say, Fletch. I'm leaving here and going back to England as soon as Trish is home from hospital.'

Fletch ignored her. He'd move heaven and earth to keep her with him and with several weeks left before Trish was due, he had time on his side.

There would be no more playing it her way.

'Before we can go forward, there's something you need to know first.'

Tess glared at him. 'There is no forward, Fletch.'

He ignored her. 'There was a woman...'

The four words free-fell into the space between them and seem to stay suspended, hovering there for an age.

When they finally landed Tess felt each one slam like a bullet straight through her heart.

Fletch had...cheated on her? 'Do you mean you—?'

'Yes,' he said, cutting her off because he couldn't bear to hear her utter his transgression aloud.

Tess stared at him. She'd known on some level just how messed up she was and that she'd been closed off and shut down and it was not fair to Fletch, but she'd never have thought in a million years he would find someone else.

Her faith in his fidelity had always been rock solid.

Fletch's stomach clenched at the look of shock on her face. She was looking at him like she had that day after the ambulance had whisked Ryan away. He wanted to reach out to her but knew her well enough to know that it wasn't the right time.

'It was at the intensive care conference I went to the weekend before we split up,' he continued, his hands shaking, his voice husky. 'She was in the bar late on the Saturday night. I couldn't sleep. She smiled at me, we talked for a while...' He shook his head. 'It was just the once... Hell, I don't even know her name. I left her room straight away afterwards, but...' he shook his head '...I couldn't believe I'd done it. Knew I'd never forgive myself. Knew that we were over...that I'd signed our marital death warrant. So when I came home on Sunday night and you asked me for a divorce, I agreed.'

Tess remembered that weekend. Remembered the

overwhelming sense of relief as he'd left, knowing she didn't have to look at him for forty-eight hours. The sudden realisation that their marriage was over. That they'd drifted too far apart.

She remembered him coming home from the conference that Sunday evening. *How could she not?* Asking for a divorce had been her first act of courage in a year.

She also remembered his lack of fight. Remembered being surprised by it even as she'd rejoiced in his capitulation.

But she hadn't demanded to know why, had just accepted it at face value, knowing she could move on in her own way, in her own time. No more listening to him talk about Ryan and what had happened, ad nauseam. No more analysis of every single detail. No more requests for her to go to counselling.

It had been a green light to deal with things her way and she'd embraced the end of her marriage as a way to begin again—far away from everything that hurt so much.

And things had been just fine—until now.

Now she had to face the fact that her husband had picked up some woman in a hotel bar while she'd been at home grieving for their son.

'Why are you telling me this?' she asked him, shaking her head as the knowledge hurt much, much more than she expected. 'Why didn't you just keep it to yourself?'

'I can't, Tess. I love you and I want you back. And this is something that's been eating at me, would continue to eat at me. It would erode any chance we had for the future.'

'So you get to feel better and unburdened and I get to feel like shit?' She lunged forward and pushed him hard in the chest. 'Gee, Fletch, thanks a lot!' She glared at him wild-eyed. 'I don't even get an orgasm to take the sting out of it!'

Fletch took a step back as his body absorbed her shove. 'I'm sorry. I'm so sorry, Tess. But would you rather we'd had sex and then I told you?'

Tess looked at him, flabbergasted. 'I'd rather you hadn't done it in the first place, you lousy, cheating bastard!' she hissed, conscious of Jean sleeping down the hall. 'Then, yes, I'd have preferred you'd kept it to yourself.'

Fletch snorted. 'Do you know most wives would have demanded to know why I did it, not why I told?'

'Well, I guess you already knew I'm not like most wives!'

He shook his head. 'You're not even curious?'

'I'm assuming that one year without sex was your personal limit and seeing as you weren't getting it from me, you got it where you could.'

Fletch's hands curled into fists as he almost roared out loud at the unfairness of her assessment. *She didn't have a clue.* Not a single clue. He turned away from her, planting his fists up high on the windows, hanging his head, fighting for control.

'Hell, Tess,' he said after a long moment or two. 'It wasn't about the sex.'

Tess turned so she was looking at his back. 'So it was love?' she scoffed, her voice ripe with sarcasm.

He waited until his temper was truly in check before he turned around again. He placed his hands behind his back and lounged against the glass, trapping them there.

'It wasn't about sex or love, Tess, it was about affection. She looked at me like I was a man,' he said in a low voice. 'An interesting man. An attractive, interest-

ing man with interesting things to say. Not as a grieving father. Or an inadequate husband. She didn't look
at me like I'd let her down. Like I'd failed her. Like I'd
killed her child.'

Tess gasped, wrapping her arms around her body to
fend off his shocking words. 'I didn't do that, Fletch.'

'She didn't flinch when I touched her, Tess,' he continued ignoring her protestation. 'She looked at me, *at
me*, Tess. Not at what I *hadn't* done but what I could do.'

He shifted, bringing his arms up to cross his chest.
'It's not an excuse for my behaviour. I was weak and it
was wrong and I've regretted it every day since. And
I'm sorry that you'd rather not know about it, but I want
to start anew with you, Tess. We've spent all this time
avoiding the hard stuff—second time round it has to
be warts and all.'

Tess couldn't even begin to assess the revelations that
had just occurred. Knowing that Fletch had indulged in
a one-night stand was mind-blowing. Hearing his rea-
sons had been shocking.

Confessing that he wanted her back was just way
too much altogether.

It was too much. It was all too much.

She was trembling but she wasn't sure if it was from
anger or shock.

She dropped her arms. 'I'm sorry too, Fletch,' she
murmured, then turned away from him and headed for
the walk-in wardrobe.

'What are you doing?' he asked as he watched her
disappear inside.

Tess grabbed the overnight bag that she'd arrived
with just over a month ago. 'I'm packing,' she said.

Fletch frowned. He pushed off the glass and strode
briskly to the large open cupboard space. She was emp-

tying the drawers he'd cleaned out for her. Grabbing her few paltry belongings off hangers.

He folded his arms. 'I thought you were staying until Trish had the baby.'

Tess steeled herself against the guilt of her broken promise. Fletch's family was not her family.

Not now. Not for a long time.

'Nope. Not any more.'

Fletch heard the finality in her voice and realised she was serious. 'Tess, don't,' he said, shoving his hands in his pockets. 'This is crazy. What about Mum? You promised you'd stay.'

Tess hardened her heart. 'That was before your little revelation tonight.'

She zipped up the bag with a vicious flick of her wrist, dragging it past him and throwing it on the bed. She went into the bathroom, clothes in hand, and threw them on. As usual she didn't bother with any make-up and she refused to look in the mirror as she gathered her paltry toiletry supplies.

She felt like she was about to shatter into a thousand pieces and she didn't want to see what that looked like. She'd made a habit of avoiding mirrors this last ten years—tonight would not be a good time to start. Her heart was pounding and her ears were ringing when she strode out two minutes later.

'Where are you going?' he demanded. 'It's the middle of the night.'

'To the airport,' she said, more calmly than she felt.

She knew she had to go now. If she waited until the morning, when both Jean and Tabby were looking at her with their big eyes, she'd knew she'd cave in.

Much easier to look into the eyes of an adulterer and walk away.

Fletch wondered if he hadn't maybe tipped her over the edge. She looked so calm and yet was acting so crazy. 'You haven't even got a flight booked,' he reasoned.

'I have a credit card.' She shrugged, picking up her watch from the bedside table and slipping it on. 'I'll get on the first airline with a flight out to London.' She shoved her feet into her shoes by the bed and grabbed her bag.

'Tess.' He put a stilling hand on her arm. 'Please, don't go. Don't run like you always do. Stay and help me work it out.'

Tess looked down at his hand. 'Don't touch me,' she warned. 'Don't you ever touch me again.'

And then she turned on her heel and marched away and she didn't look back and she didn't stop until she got to the safety of her car, where she locked all the doors and burst into tears.

CHAPTER ELEVEN

Six weeks later Tess was just about cried out—talk about the straw that broke the camel's back!

She'd cried big, fat, silent tears for twenty-four hours solid on her plane trip home. The air hostesses had been so concerned about her that three of them had surrounded her outside the loos about four hours into the flight and asked her what was wrong.

'My husband cheated on me,' she'd told them, because it had been easier than the whole truth and it had hurt too much to keep it inside any longer.

Before she'd known it and in a startling display of female solidarity, she'd been whisked into business class for a little more privacy. Silent tears had rolled down her face as she'd thanked them.

She'd cried louder tears in her car, hurtling down the motorway towards Devon. She'd cried herself to sleep, she cried when she woke up and she cried at work. Hell, she'd even cried at the supermarket yesterday when a baby sitting in a trolley had smiled a dribbly smile at her.

She doubted she'd ever cried this much in her life. Not even in those first two months after Ryan had died.

Even sitting here right now snuggled in her pink polar fleece dressing gown in front of her fire on a chilly November night cradling a photo of Ryan in her lap, she could feel the tears pricking at her eyes again.

She shut them. 'Please, no,' she whispered. 'No more.'

The phone rang and her eyes flew open. The muscles in her neck tensed as they'd formed the habit of doing every time it rang since she'd returned home. Her answering machine was full of messages from Fletch, who had taken to ringing several times a day for the first couple of weeks.

Wanting to talk. Wanting her to understand. Wanting her to come back.

The last time had been two weeks ago when he'd rung to tell her that Trish had given birth to a bouncing baby girl and he was an uncle again. Her heart had swelled with joy and happiness for Trish. She'd been standing right beside the phone, listening to the message as he'd left it, and she'd almost picked it up that time to share the occasion with him.

But she'd gone to bed and cried instead.

The answering machine clicked in and the tension oozed from her muscles as old Dulcie Frobisher, the secretary of the historical society, informed her she was sending Peter around with some jam she'd made because she knew how much Tess enjoyed it.

Tess rolled her eyes at the message, knowing that Dulcie also thought that her great-nephew, who after years of frustrating bachelorhood had finally come out of the closet three months ago, just needed the love of a good woman and that Tess, being practically the only single woman in town in his age bracket, filled that criterion.

Tess was used to well-intentioned villagers trying

to fix her up with their sons, grandsons, nephews and widowed neighbours.

She looked down at her wedding ring, which seemed to mock her in the firelight. It may have been a force field to keep men at bay but she'd always believed in what it had represented.

Love, commitment, fidelity.

A knock interrupted her thoughts and she gave an inward groan. Dulcie must have nagged the poor man into action immediately because she just didn't get visitors at eight o'clock at night. She grimaced as she stood, mentally preparing herself for the encounter. She flipped on the outside light as she pulled open the door.

'Hi, Tess,' Pete said apologetically, holding out three jars of jam.

'Hi, Pete, thanks. Dulcie just called.' She took the jars from him. 'Do you want to come in?' she asked, hoping sincerely that he didn't.

He shook his head. 'No, I'd better get back. I have some pots firing.'

But he seemed reluctant to leave so she asked, 'How are things?'

'About the same.' He sighed.

'You know, you really need to go and live in London for a while, Pete,' she said gently. 'Gay men are pretty thin on the ground in this neck of the woods.'

He nodded glumly. 'I know. But I can't leave Dulcie. Or the art gallery. And I'm sure I'm way too country bumpkin for the big smoke.'

Tess put her hand on his arm. 'You're a nice man, Pete, and very nice-looking to boot. You're smart and articulate and arty. Any man would be lucky to have you.'

Pete gave a half-laugh. 'You're good for my ego,

Tess,' he said as he leaned in to kiss her on the cheek and sweep her into a hug.

It felt good to relax in a man's arms with no expectations and she hung on for a little longer than she normally would until a sudden harsh cough behind them had them both leaping apart guiltily.

It was Fletch.

Standing on her garden path, his strong, beautiful jaw clenched tight, his hands jammed in the pockets of a warm, heavy coat.

He looked from Pete to Tess then back to Pete again.

'Hello, Tess.'

Tess blinked. 'Fletcher?'

Fletch threw a steely glare towards Peter. 'Yes.'

'What are you doing here?' she asked dazedly.

'We need to talk,' he said tersely, his gaze not leaving the other man.

Peter took one look at the magnificent, tight-lipped guy staring him down and concluded that if this was a London man, then he truly did need to get there pronto. 'Is everything okay?' he asked Tess, dragging his eyes away from the stranger. 'Do you want me to stay?'

Tess could see Fletch bristling and came out of her daze, stepping in before things got any more tense. She introduced the two men—Fletch as her ex-husband and Peter as a jam-bearing friend—and assured a rather disappointed Peter she'd be fine.

She saw Fletch through Peter's eyes and sympathised. He cut a dashing figure in his heavy wool coat, which only seemed to emphasise the power of his chest, the breadth of his shoulders. The alcove light caught the streaks of grey at his temples that had been tousled to salon perfection by the brisk November breeze. The three-day growth looked shaggy and touchable. He looked tired. But solid and warm and sexy.

Very, very sexy.

'Tell Dulcie I'll ring her tomorrow,' Tess said as Peter turned to go.

Fletch watched the man retreat down the path and out the gate, giving Tess a wave as he turned left down the street. Even though he was obviously gay, Fletch felt a spike of jealousy. He didn't want *any* man's hands around her unless they were his!

He turned back and looked at her, capturing her gaze. She looked so good in her pink polar fleece he wanted to sweep her up in his arms and bury his face in it. But it was freezing out here and there were things to say.

'Can I come in?'

This was not the way that Tess had expected her day would finish up. She didn't usually hug gay men on her doorstep or have her ex-husband turn up out of the blue.

But, then, not a lot had been normal lately.

'Sure,' she said, standing aside.

He brushed past her, ducking his head to fit under her low cottage doorway, and every cell in her body went onto high alert. He shrugged out of his coat to reveal charcoal slacks and a round-necked, fine-knit sweater in navy blue, which clung to every muscle in his chest, and those same recalcitrant cells went into overdrive.

But the full lights inside accentuated rather than softened the lines around his eyes and mouth and he looked every day of his forty years.

'You look awful,' she said.

'Thank you.' He grimaced as the cosy atmosphere wrapped him in a big warm hug even if her observation hadn't. 'Don't suppose you have proper coffee? I've just got off possibly the longest transpacific flight in living human memory with a grizzly baby behind me and a man who sounded like he had whooping cough in front of me.'

Tess smiled despite her state of confusion. 'Sure,' she said again, and headed for the kitchen. She made them both a cup while Fletch watched her with brooding silvery-green eyes.

She passed him a steaming mug and led him over to the lounge area where a three-seater couch and a coffee table stood a safe distance away from the glowing fireplace.

She sat at one end and he at the other. 'How's Trish and the baby?' she asked, because it was easier to start with the inane stuff.

Fletch took a reviving sip of coffee, shutting his eyes as the caffeine buzzed into his system. 'Great. She went into labour at thirty-six weeks but the obstetrician was happy with that.'

He fished around in his trouser pocket and pulled out his phone. He touched the screen a few times and pulled up the pictures of baby Katrina and handed it to Tess.

Tess swiped her finger across the screen, smiling at the pics of Trish and Doug and their daughter. One of Christopher holding his sister very carefully scrolled up and Tess felt her heart contract.

'You can tell they're brother and sister,' she murmured as Katrina's two cowlicks became more evident next to her brother's. 'Christopher looks no worse for wear,' she mused, examining his sweet little face for signs of long-term damage.

Tess had learned from one of Fletch's many phone messages that Christopher had been discharged from hospital two days after his seizure and that nothing had turned up on any of the investigations the hospital had run.

'Oh, yeah.' Fletch smiled. 'Back to normal.'

The next one that scrolled up was of Fletch holding his little niece. He was smiling but she knew him well enough to see that it didn't reach his eyes.

He'd always wanted a daughter.

Then it was Jean's turn. She looked fit and happy but Tess could tell from her eyes that she didn't feel any kind of connection with the little bundle in her arms. Not like the hundreds of pictures they'd had of Jean holding Ryan as a newborn, where her love and pride and awe had shone from her eyes like a beacon.

'How's your mum?' Tess asked, touching Jean's cheek with her finger.

'She's okay, I guess. Not as settled as when you were there, although Tabby has helped enormously.'

Tess could tell that Fletch was trying to keep the accusation out of his voice. 'I'm sorry,' she said, looking up at him, 'for leaving you in the lurch.'

Fletch shrugged. He couldn't really blame her. 'I managed.' It had been a huge juggling act but somehow he'd got through the last six weeks. 'She went back with Trish yesterday. Or...' he looked at his watch '...the day before...whatever the time is now.'

Tess gave a half-smile. Jet-lag and time zones always left her at sixes and sevens. She handed him back his phone and they sat and watched the fire without saying anything for a minute.

'I'm sorry too,' Fletch said. 'For a lot of things, but especially for not coming sooner. I wanted to follow you... I would have followed you but...'

Tess nodded. She'd flown to the other side of the world because running away was what she did best but part of it was also about knowing he was stuck at home with Jean and couldn't follow.

But he was here now.

He'd come after her this time.

Last time she'd asked him to leave her alone and he had. This time he'd come anyway.

Fletch put his mug down on the coffee table, feeling the boost of the caffeine bolster his nerve. He'd made a vow that he wouldn't come back to Australia until Tess was with him, and the time to make his pitch was now.

He noticed a face-down photo frame near where he placed his mug and he picked it up and turned it over. A close-up of Ryan stared back at him, his green eyes sparkling. Not even a party hat at a jaunty angle was able to disguise how his blond hair stuck up on top from that impossible double cowlick.

He'd taken the picture at Ryan's first birthday party.

He looked at Tess, surprised—she'd taken all the photos of Ryan down two months after he'd died, declaring she just couldn't look at them any more.

It had been as if he'd never existed.

'Reminiscing?'

She nodded. 'I've been looking at that picture for six weeks. It doesn't hurt to look at it any more.'

'That's good,' he said tentatively, encouraged that Tess finally seemed to be facing things instead of locking them all away.

Had their argument the night she'd left been the catalyst?

Tess looked into the depths of her milky coffee. 'You never blamed me,' she murmured. Then she looked at him. 'Not once.'

Fletch frowned then scooted to the middle cushion, folding one leg under him till he was turned side on in the lounge. He placed a hand on her arm. 'It wasn't your fault, Tess.'

She shook her head as tears welled in her eyes and rolled down her cheeks. 'I fell asleep, Fletch. I was supposed to be watching him and I fell asleep.'

Fletch had finished a run of five night duties and had been sleeping in the bedroom. Normally Tess would have had Ryan outside to keep him quiet for Fletch or even taken him out, but it had rained quite heavily overnight and had still been drizzling that morning. And she'd felt too ill herself to go anywhere. So she'd set him up with a DVD on low and his building blocks on the lounge-room floor. At some stage she'd drifted off sitting upright in the lounge chair as she'd watched over him.

'Tess, you'd been up all night with him, teething. You'd had only marginally more sleep than me for the three previous nights and you had a really bad migraine that you'd taken something for. You were exhausted.'

Fletch had offered to stay up with Ryan for a few hours while Tess had got some sleep but she had assured him she'd be fine and he *had* been very grateful. He'd been so tired he hadn't been able to see straight.

Normally in that kind of situation they would have had Jean come and look after Ryan but she'd been going off to the coast for the day so they'd decided they'd tag-team and manage between the two of them.

'He was shut in the lounge room with you,' Fletch continued. 'You had no reason not to think he was safe. If *I'd* fixed the dicky latch on the door you'd been nagging me to do for a week, he wouldn't have been able to get out.'

Tess shook her head, wiping at the tears. 'I should

have turned the bucket over the day before. Put it away like I always did.'

Tess had been playing with Ryan the afternoon before in the sand pit. She'd pulled the deep bucket out of the shed because Ryan had loved to fill it with sand. But because his clumsy toddling kept knocking it over and he was becoming frustrated, she'd dug it into the sand a bit and wedged it into the angle of wooden framework to stabilise it.

And then the phone had rung and they'd raced to answer it so it wouldn't wake Fletch but it had and they'd all had some family time together before Fletch had gone off to work again and she'd forgotten all about the bucket in the sand pit.

'Tess, you weren't to know it was going to pour down with rain that night. It was an accident, Tess, a freak accident. A freak set of circumstances. Don't you see we can go back and forth for ever like this? You shouldn't have fallen asleep. I should have fixed the door. We should have put the bucket away. I should have done a better resus job.'

He cupped her cheek and swiped at a tear with his thumb. 'At some stage we've got to forgive ourselves.'

Tess raised her hand to cover his. 'He died, Fletcher. Our little boy died.' She looked into his eyes. 'I keep wishing I could go back to that day and change just one thing, you know?' she implored him. 'I'd stay awake. Because then none of that other stuff matters—if I had been watching him, everything else would be moot.'

Fletch couldn't bear the pain in her amber eyes. He would have given anything to take it from her. But he knew that by finally talking about it she was taking the first steps towards expunging it herself. Steps towards living a full life again instead of the half-life she'd allowed herself tucked away in the middle of nowhere.

He pulled her towards him and wrapped her up tight. 'The door,' he said against her temple. 'I should have fixed that door when you first complained about it.'

Tess heard her own anguish echoed in his words and when the sob rose in her chest she didn't try to stop it. She let it out. And the low wail that followed it. The gut-wrenching wail that cut like razors on its way out but instead of leaving her bloodied it left her feeling infinitely lighter.

Fletch held her while she sobbed. It was the first time apart from at the hospital and the funeral that she'd let him hold her while she'd cried. His own tears mingled with hers as they finally grieved for their son together.

Tess didn't know how long she cried for or even where the tears had come from, considering how much she'd already cried these past six weeks. But she did know that she felt better for it and that it had felt right to share her tears with Fletch.

She eventually lifted her head from his shoulder. She was surprised to see his eyes also rimmed with red.

She smiled at him as she gently fluttered her fingers over his eyelids. 'I'm sorry,' she murmured.

He shook his head, his eyes closed. 'Don't be.'

She traced the slopes of his cheekbones down to the corners of his mouth. 'Why didn't you tell me about… the other woman? Back then? Was I that fragile?'

Fletch opened his eyes. 'Yes, you were. But mostly…' he shrugged '…I was just ashamed and sick to my stomach over my actions. I could barely face you. I certainly didn't feel like I deserved you after what I'd done. When you gave me the chance to end it I grabbed it with both hands. It seemed like a better alternative than having to confess.'

Tess traced his bottom lip with her thumb. 'I guess that couldn't have been an easy thing to tell.'

Fletch felt the stroke of her thumb right down to his groin. 'You don't seem so mad about it any more,' he said tentatively.

Tess nodded realising he was right. 'I've done a lot of soul-searching since coming home. I wasn't easy to live with, Fletch. You tried so hard…every day…you were so patient with me. But I was so caught up in my denial stage, avoiding even the slightest mention of Ryan, that I forgot you were grieving too. That you needed someone to lean on as well. I don't blame you for finding a little solace somewhere else for a few hours.'

She dropped her hand into her lap. 'Don't get me wrong, it hurts…but I need to own my part in that.'

Fletch picked up her hand from her lap and pressed a kiss to the back of it. 'I'm sorry. I'm so sorry. I didn't just stop loving you because you were done with me, Tess, but we went to bed each night and there was this great divide between us that I just couldn't breach, no matter how I tried.'

Tess nodded, swallowing a lump that had risen to her throat. She'd been so inside herself she hadn't realised just how much he'd been suffering too.

'But I want us back together, Tess.' He raised her chin so they were looking into each other's eyes. 'I think you still love me and I don't want to live any more of my life without you in it.'

Tess nodded. He was right. She did still love him. She didn't need a clanging of gongs or a light bulb over her head to know it. It hummed quietly in every cell, as it always had. She just hadn't been listening.

And the truth was their marriage hadn't ended because they'd fallen out of love—it had ended because they'd given up on that love when everything else had got too hard.

'I do, Fletch. I do love you.' She sniffed and wiped at yet another tear. 'But do you really think we deserve a second shot when we screwed it up so badly the first time? Do you think we can truly be happy?'

Fletch cradled her face, pushing his long fingers into her hair. 'Yes, Tess, yes. Everyone deserves a second chance. I'm not pretending that the road ahead is going to be all roses and sunshine. We need counselling, Tess, both together and separately. We have a decade's worth of guilt and grief that needs to be talked about and I imagine that's going to be pretty harrowing at times. I know you've never wanted to talk about this before but we can't go on like that again. We have to do it differently this time round.'

Tess could see the love and determination mingling in his silvery-green gaze. 'I don't want to walk around with this stuff inside me any more, Fletch. I'm so tired of carrying it around.'

Fletch leaned in and brushed his mouth against hers. Finally he felt that everything was going to be all right.

Tess pulled back from his kiss, a swell of emotion blooming in her chest. He looked warm and solid and calm and she needed him more than ever. 'I love you,' she murmured.

Fletch smiled. 'Then the rest will come,' he whispered, claiming her mouth once again.

And for the first time in a decade Tess looked forward to the future.

* * * * *

Mills & Boon® Hardback
August 2012

ROMANCE

Contract with Consequences	Miranda Lee
The Sheikh's Last Gamble	Trish Morey
The Man She Shouldn't Crave	Lucy Ellis
The Girl He'd Overlooked	Cathy Williams
A Tainted Beauty	Sharon Kendrick
One Night With The Enemy	Abby Green
The Dangerous Jacob Wilde	Sandra Marton
His Last Chance at Redemption	Michelle Conder
The Hidden Heart of Rico Rossi	Kate Hardy
Marrying the Enemy	Nicola Marsh
Mr Right, Next Door!	Barbara Wallace
The Cowboy Comes Home	Patricia Thayer
The Rancher's Housekeeper	Rebecca Winters
Her Outback Rescuer	Marion Lennox
Monsoon Wedding Fever	Shoma Narayanan
If the Ring Fits...	Jackie Braun
Sydney Harbour Hospital: Ava's Re-Awakening	Carol Marinelli
How To Mend A Broken Heart	Amy Andrews

MEDICAL

Falling for Dr Fearless	Lucy Clark
The Nurse He Shouldn't Notice	Susan Carlisle
Every Boy's Dream Dad	Sue MacKay
Return of the Rebel Surgeon	Connie Cox

ROMANCE

A Deal at the Altar	Lynne Graham
Return of the Moralis Wife	Jacqueline Baird
Gianni's Pride	Kim Lawrence
Undone by His Touch	Annie West
The Cattle King's Bride	Margaret Way
New York's Finest Rebel	Trish Wylie
The Man Who Saw Her Beauty	Michelle Douglas
The Last Real Cowboy	Donna Alward
The Legend of de Marco	Abby Green
Stepping out of the Shadows	Robyn Donald
Deserving of His Diamonds?	Melanie Milburne

HISTORICAL

The Scandalous Lord Lanchester	Anne Herries
Highland Rogue, London Miss	Margaret Moore
His Compromised Countess	Deborah Hale
The Dragon and the Pearl	Jeannie Lin
Destitute On His Doorstep	Helen Dickson

MEDICAL

Sydney Harbour Hospital: Lily's Scandal	Marion Lennox
Sydney Harbour Hospital: Zoe's Baby	Alison Roberts
Gina's Little Secret	Jennifer Taylor
Taming the Lone Doc's Heart	Lucy Clark
The Runaway Nurse	Dianne Drake
The Baby Who Saved Dr Cynical	Connie Cox

0712 GEN STD LP

Mills & Boon® Hardback

September 2012

ROMANCE

Unlocking her Innocence	Lynne Graham
Santiago's Command	Kim Lawrence
His Reputation Precedes Him	Carole Mortimer
The Price of Retribution	Sara Craven
Just One Last Night	Helen Brooks
The Greek's Acquisition	Chantelle Shaw
The Husband She Never Knew	Kate Hewitt
When Only Diamonds Will Do	Lindsay Armstrong
The Couple Behind the Headlines	Lucy King
The Best Mistake of Her Life	Aimee Carson
The Valtieri Baby	Caroline Anderson
Slow Dance with the Sheriff	Nikki Logan
Bella's Impossible Boss	Michelle Douglas
The Tycoon's Secret Daughter	Susan Meier
She's So Over Him	Joss Wood
Return of the Last McKenna	Shirley Jump
Once a Playboy...	Kate Hardy
Challenging the Nurse's Rules	Janice Lynn

MEDICAL

Her Motherhood Wish	Anne Fraser
A Bond Between Strangers	Scarlet Wilson
The Sheikh and the Surrogate Mum	Meredith Webber
Tamed by her Brooding Boss	Joanna Neil

Mills & Boon® Large Print

September 2012

ROMANCE

A Vow of Obligation	Lynne Graham
Defying Drakon	Carole Mortimer
Playing the Greek's Game	Sharon Kendrick
One Night in Paradise	Maisey Yates
Valtieri's Bride	Caroline Anderson
The Nanny Who Kissed Her Boss	Barbara McMahon
Falling for Mr Mysterious	Barbara Hannay
The Last Woman He'd Ever Date	Liz Fielding
His Majesty's Mistake	Jane Porter
Duty and the Beast	Trish Morey
The Darkest of Secrets	Kate Hewitt

HISTORICAL

Lady Priscilla's Shameful Secret	Christine Merrill
Rake with a Frozen Heart	Marguerite Kaye
Miss Cameron's Fall from Grace	Helen Dickson
Society's Most Scandalous Rake	Isabelle Goddard
The Taming of the Rogue	Amanda McCabe

MEDICAL

Falling for the Sheikh She Shouldn't	Fiona McArthur
Dr Cinderella's Midnight Fling	Kate Hardy
Brought Together by Baby	Margaret McDonagh
One Month to Become a Mum	Louisa George
Sydney Harbour Hospital: Luca's Bad Girl	Amy Andrews
The Firebrand Who Unlocked His Heart	Anne Fraser

0812 GEN STD LP